We all stared in horror as the monster appeared in the sky. It had the head of a donkey. A mean, vicious donkey.

"It's Typhon!" cried Hera. "That monster Hyperion told us about!"

Hissing and roaring, Typhon swooped down.

Our godly powers kicked into high gear. Hera instantly changed herself into a white cow and galloped off toward Egypt. Apollo morphed into a crow and flapped off after her. Artemis became a wild cat; Aphrodite, a boar; and Dionysus, a goat. They all turned into beasts and ran away as fast as they could.

And the brave and mighty Zeus? Do you think he turned into a lion? A mighty ram? A bull elephant, maybe? Wrong, wrong, wrong! Zeus turned himself into a chipmunk, and dove down the nearest hole.

I didn't change into anything, but I did put on my helmet of invisibility, and I ran over to the chipmunk hole. "Zeus! We have to drive Typhon away! We have to fight this monster! Come out!"

"Nothing doing," Zeus squeaked from inside the hole.

# Have a Hot Time, HADES!

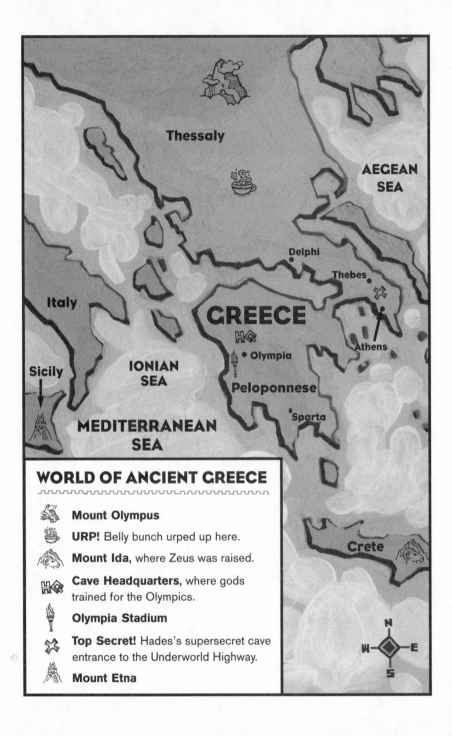

**Thessaly**

**AEGEAN SEA**

**Italy**

Delphi

Thebes

**GREECE**

Athens

Olympia

**IONIAN SEA**

**Peloponnese**

**Sicily**

Sparta

**MEDITERRANEAN SEA**

Crete

## WORLD OF ANCIENT GREECE

**Mount Olympus**

**URP!** Belly bunch urped up here.

**Mount Ida,** where Zeus was raised.

**Cave Headquarters,** where gods trained for the Olympics.

**Olympia Stadium**

**Top Secret!** Hades's supersecret cave entrance to the Underworld Highway.

**Mount Etna**

BOOK **MYTH-O-MANIA** ONE

# Have a Hot Time, HADES!

By
Kate McMullan

Illustrated by
David LaFleur

VOLO

HYPERION
New York

Printed in the United States of America
First Edition
1 3 5 7 9 10 8 6 4 2

ISBN 0-7868-1664-3 (paperback)
ISBN 0-7868-0857-8 (hardcover)

Library of Congress Cataloging-in-Publication Data on file.

Visit www.volobooks.com

For Mr. Mathews, Ms. Cross,
and all the brilliant kids at Grace Church School

⊓_⊓_⊓_⊓_⊓_⊓_⊓_

With many burnt offerings of gratitude
to my muse-editor, Susan Chang,
and to my agent, Holly McGoddess

## Prologue

Call me Hades.

My full name—His Royal Lowness, Lord of the Dead, King Hades—is a bit of a mouthful.

I rule the Underworld. The ghosts of the dead travel down to dwell in my kingdom. If they were good in life, they get to go to an eternal rock concert, where really great bands play on and on forever. The ghosts of the not-so-good? They have to wander around, trying to memorize an endless list of really hard spelling words. And the ghosts of the wicked? You *don't* want to know.

It's my job to make sure everything in the

Underworld runs smoothly. After a hard day, I like to go home to the palace with my dog. Don't I, Cerberus? Yes, that's my good old boy, boy, boy. (He has three heads, and he hates it when I leave one out.)

I had my palace totally wired millennia ago with a super cable hookup with all the premium stuff. Plus Channel Earth and HB-Olympus, so I can keep an eye on what's happening up above.

I have a great library, too. You think the Big-Fat-Book-of-the-Month Club doesn't know how to find me down here? Last month their featured selection was *The Big Fat Book of Greek Myths*. I knew all the stories, of course, but I thought it might be a fun read. So I sat down in my La-Z-God, shifted into recline, and started in. I couldn't believe the nonsense I was reading! Take a look for yourself—go on, read it!

At first, there was only darkness. Then Mother Earth, called Gaia, and Father Sky appeared. They had twelve giant Titan children.

The youngest, Cronus, became father of the greatest god of all time, the brave and mighty Zeus.

Brave and mighty Zeus? Ha! Chickenhearted Zeus, is more like it. Okay, he *is* officially Ruler of the Universe, but that's only because he cheated at cards.

The more I read, the madder I got. The stories were all wrong. Not a single one was told the way it really happened.

But I knew what the problem was. My little brother Zeus had been messing with the myths. He'd scratched out all the parts that didn't fit with his own overblown idea of himself as Supreme Thunder God, Ruler of the Universe. He'd added things, too.

Lots of things! All the stories about him hurling lightning bolts? The guy is so out of shape he couldn't hurl a lightning *bug*. And the bit about him being so great that he was crowned with a laurel wreath? Trust me, he only wears that thing to hide his bald spot. What a myth-o-maniac! (That's old-Greek-speak for "liar.")

Finally I slammed the book shut. There was only one thing for me to do. I had to write a book of my own to set the record straight.

Writing a book was harder than I expected. But I was lucky. My kingdom is loaded with ghost writers! Once I put them to work, the whole thing was a snap.

Now, for the first time ever, you can read the myths the way they *really* happened.

So move over, Zeus.

Make way for me, Hades!

## Chapter I

# HOTHEAD DAD

Way, way back—so long ago that time and space and triple-digit division problems had only just been invented—a race of giants called Titans ruled the earth. They were so big that their mama Gaia, also known as Mother Earth, made mountains as their thrones. Where do you think the word "titanic" comes from, anyway? Right—from the immortal Titans.

Cronus was the youngest Titan, and Mama Gaia was just crazy about him. After he was born, Mama Gaia decided that she and Sky Daddy would never have a more perfect son, so she declared that no more Titans would be born, ever.

Mama Gaia loved giving young Cronus presents. She gave him a golden girdle (old-speak for "belt"). She gave him a silver sickle (old-speak for "Weedwacker"), which he hung from his golden girdle. And she gave him his very own kingdom on top of Mount Olympus, a mountain which was one hundred times taller than any other mountain on earth.

Mama Gaia spoiled him rotten.

From the top of Mount Olympus, Cronus ruled over all the other Titans. He ruled over all the beasts and the mortals on earth at that time, too. Cronus was the Ruler of the Universe, the Big Enchilada. Everyone called him "O Mighty Cronus!"

I called him Dad.

My mom, Rhea, was a Titan, too. She was tickled pink to be married to the Ruler of the Universe. Because no more Titans were to be born, Rhea knew that her children would be little gods. Well, not as little as mortals, but not too much bigger. Still, she couldn't wait to start her own royal family. Everything might have worked out fine if it hadn't been for that prophecy.

It seems that Dad was not content to be Ruler of

the Universe. He also wanted to know the future. So he went to visit a seer—an old, blind fortune-teller. He sat down on a hill and asked the seer to tell him about his future children.

"O Mighty Cronus!" the seer said. "You shall have six children!"

"Ah, six!" said Dad. "That is good!"

"O Mighty Cronus!" said the seer. "Three of your children shall be sons. And three shall be daughters!"

"Ah, three of each!" said Dad. "That is good!"

"O Mighty Cronus!" said the seer. "One of the children shall be mightier than the father and one day shall overthrow him!"

"Ah, mightier!" said Dad. "That is—wait a minute. *I* am the father. What are you saying? That one of my children shall overthrow ME?"

"The future grows cloudy," the old seer muttered. He knew better than to answer *that* question.

"I'll slay them all!" Cronus shouted. "No one shall be mightier than mighty Cronus!"

"Your children shall be immortal," the old seer pointed out. "You cannot slay them."

"Humph," said Cronus. "Well, I'll think of something."

Not long after that, I was born. I was tiny—not much bigger than Mom's fist. Mom wrapped me up nice and tight in a swaddling blanket with my name stitched on it, as was the custom. Only my face stuck out. She proudly carried me to my father.

"Behold, O Mighty Cronus!" Mom said. "Here is Hades, your firstborn son! Is he not a handsome little baby god? Look at his teensy dimples!"

Mom handed me to Dad. Dad held me up close to his face. Mom thought he was going to kiss me. Wrong! Dad opened up his giant mouth, shoved me in, and—*GULP!* He swallowed me whole.

I half remember sliding down a slippery tunnel, then *THUMP!* I landed in a huge dark space. Somewhere outside, I heard Mom shrieking. Dad started laughing, which bounced me all over the place inside his stomach. He couldn't get over his clever plan to keep me from becoming mightier than he was. And there was nothing Mom could do about it.

So it was that I spent my early days inside the cave of Dad's stomach. It was dark, as I said. But after a while my eyes adjusted to it. The thing I never got used to was how damp and sticky it was, especially at mealtimes.

Like all immortal beings, Dad needed to eat ambrosia and drink nectar in order to stay peppy and strong. Ambrosia is something like angel-food cake with orange frosting. Nectar is like ancient Greek apple juice. So when I say sticky, I mean *sticky*.

But the worst of it was, there was nothing to do down there. So I thought up ways to make Dad miserable. I kicked him. I punched him. I jumped up and down for hours. If I jumped hard enough, I gave Dad the hiccups. But I'm not sure who suffered the most, Dad or me. I got tossed around with every *hic*.

Then one day—or was it night? impossible to tell, down in that gut—I was taking a little snooze when, *THUMP!* Something landed beside me. It was a wrapped-up bundle. I picked it up and undid the wrappings. Inside was my baby brother, Poseidon.

Dad was up to his tricks again.

For Poseidon's sake, I was sorry that Dad had swallowed him. But I was happy to have company. I taught Poseidon to kick and punch and jump along with me. We tried our best to give Dad some really serious stomach problems. But Cronus was just too big and too tough. Nothing bothered him.

One day—or it could have been night—Dad chugged down lots more nectar than usual. Talk about a flood! The whole place turned into a lake.

"Come on, Po!" I grabbed my brother's arm and tried to pull him to high ground.

But Po yanked himself away from me.

"Ye-hoo!" he cried as he leaped, grabbing his knees tight to his chest, and plunged into Lake Nectar.

*KER-SPLASH!*

I got soaked.

Po's head quickly popped up out of the lake.

"Did you see that, Hades?" he yelled up to me. "I call it 'the cannonball'!"

"I call it disgusting." Nectar dripped from my hair into my eyes. *Yecch!*

Po started paddling around in the sticky stuff. "And I call this the 'doggie paddle'!"

He stayed in and swam until all the nectar had been digested.

In the years that followed, my three sisters slid down Dad's throat.

First Hestia. *THUMP!*

Then Demeter. *THUMP!*

And finally, Hera. *THUMP!*

Every time a new baby came down the chute, I heard Mom out there, screaming and yelling. Clearly she was not one bit happy with Dad's plan to keep his children from overthrowing him.

Dad's gut was so big that it wasn't crowded, even with five of us down there. Of course, every once in a while, we got on each other's nerves. Po was always trying to organize swimming meets. Hestia was always tidying up the place. Hera ordered the rest of us around, nonstop. We started calling her "the Boss"—but not to her face. Even then it didn't pay to get on the wrong side of Hera. But Demeter was definitely the weirdest. She was always going on and on about wanting to plant a little vegetable garden.

But, hey, we five were family. We grew up in Dad's belly together.

Then one night—or possibly day—*THUMP!*

"A new baby!" cried Po.

We all rushed over to where the baby had landed.

Po picked it up. He began unwrapping its swaddling blanket.

That's when I noticed something odd.

I didn't hear Mom outside, crying and yelling.

Suddenly, Po gasped. "This is no baby!" he cried. "Dad has swallowed a stone!"

Sure enough, in his arms, Po held a big, smooth, baby-size stone.

"You know," I said, as I looked at that stone, "I think Mom has finally come up with a plan of her own."

"Yes!" cried Demeter. "She wants us to plant a rock garden!"

"Uh . . . not exactly," I said. "Mom's fooled Dad. He thinks he's swallowed another baby. But really Mom switched the baby for this stone."

My brother and sisters nodded. And we all understood that somewhere out in the world, a baby god was growing up.

At the time, I was glad for the baby. Glad that one of us had escaped Dad's big gulp.

But that was before I'd met my little brother Zeus.

# Chapter II

## ULTRABRIGHT MOM

That stone became our plaything. Hey, when you have no toys, no TV, no bikes, no scooters, no dogs, no cats, not even a gerbil, you'd be surprised at how much fun you can have with a stone.

Po liked to throw it into Lake Nectar, then dive in and pull it out again. Hestia enjoyed polishing it. Demeter could often be found trying to find a way to plant it. And all of us, except Demeter, liked to kick it around. We invented a game we called "kickstone," where we divided into teams and tried to kick the stone into the other team's territory.

That's what we were doing the day—and it

*was* day—we heard *GLUG, GLUG, GLUG!*

"Dad's hitting the nectar again," Hera called. "Places!"

My sisters and I backed up against Dad's stomach wall. We braced ourselves for the flood of sticky liquid we knew would soon come rushing down his throat. As usual, Po ran over and assumed a bodysurfing pose under Dad's esophagus. He loved trying to catch that first big nectary wave.

I sniffed. "What's that awful smell?"

"Ew!" said Demeter. "Rotten nectar!"

Hestia started whimpering about how hard it would be to get rid of a foul odor in a closed-in space.

The smell turned quickly to a major stink. Then—*WHOOSH!* A torrent of the nastiest liquid imaginable cascaded down Dad's gullet. In no time, we were up to our necks in the stuff.

The glop didn't just sit there, either. It foamed and bubbled. Then it began churning, spinning around faster and faster, turning Dad's stomach into a giant whirlpool. It started sucking us down!

"Scissor kick! Scissor kick!" Po yelled. "Tread water! Heads high!"

We fought to keep our heads up as the smelly fluid sloshed over us. The whole place shook with Dad's moans and groans. Then the walls of his stomach started clenching like a giant fist. With every clench, a wave of the sour juice flew up Dad's throat. I don't know what happened next because the whirlpool sucked me down. It spun me around. Then suddenly, SPURT! I was catapulted up, up, up, up Dad's slimy gullet and—*BLECCHH!*—spat out into the world.

I landed on a pile of my brother and sisters. We all blinked and squinted in the daylight, the first we'd seen since our births. As we tried to untangle ourselves from each other, I figured out what had happened. Dad had just barfed. The big lug was lying above us on a hilltop, holding his stomach and wailing.

As soon as the five of us had sorted out whose feet were whose, we stood up. Demeter picked up the stone, and we ran down the hill, away from Dad. None of us wanted to take a chance on being swallowed again.

"Where are we?" asked Hera when we reached the bottom of the hill.

"You're in Greece!" came a voice from above us.

We looked around. Standing on a hill behind us was a young god. He wore a white tunic and a bronze breastplate. A sword hung from his girdle.

The guy was grinning.

"I am Zeus, your brother!" he said as he walked down the hill toward us.

Ah, so this was the god Mom had saved when she gave Dad the stone. I noticed that Zeus was bigger than the rest of us. All those years down in Dad's gut must have stunted our growth.

"It was I who rescued you," Zeus said. "You may thank me now."

We all muttered our thanks.

But really, couldn't Zeus have waited a few minutes before asking us to thank him? Here we were, newly thrown up into the world, stinking to high heaven, blind as bats in the blazing sunlight, and wearing only the tattered remains of our swaddling clothes. We needed a few minutes to pull ourselves together.

"Look!" Po cried suddenly. "A stream! Last one in is a rotten egg!"

Po cannonballed into the cool, clear water. The

rest of us were right on his heels. Ahh! Unless you've spent a few thousand years down in someone's belly, you have no idea how good a clear, clean stream can feel. Or how fine it is to breathe fresh air. And did it ever feel great not to be eternally sticky!

Zeus kept calling, "Get out! Come hear the tale of how I saved you!"

But we ignored him and stayed in that stream until we were good and ready to climb out. Then we lay in the sun to dry. Dry—what a concept! It was paradise, until Zeus ran over and started yakking about himself.

"See, Mom fooled Dad into swallowing a wrapped-up stone," Zeus said. "Then Mom rushed me to a cave on the island of Crete and hid me there where I was raised by a Fairy Goat and a band of nymphs who did whatever I told them to. They gave me this sword."

Zeus held up his sword and started banging it on his breastplate, which he called his aegis. It made a loud clank.

"The Fairy Goat gave me this aegis," Zeus continued. "No sword or arrow can pierce it. So nothing can ever hurt me as long as I have on my aegis."

"Cool," said Hera. "Can I try it on?"

"Not a chance," said Zeus. "Now, here's how I rescued you. First, I found all these stinky herbs. When Dad sat down on a little mountain this morning to have his nectar tea, I snuck the herbs into his cup. He drank the tea, and *URP!*"

"Nice work," said Po. "Thanks!"

"Yeah." Zeus nodded. "You guys owe me, big time."

As we sat there, a huge ball of bright light appeared suddenly in front of us. And out of the glow stepped a giant raven-haired Titaness.

"Mom!" we cried all at the same time.

"Oh, my little godlings!" Rhea clasped her hands to her heart. "I knew you'd know me, even after all these years!"

Talk about a family reunion. Hugs. Kisses. Tears. The works.

Mom rummaged around in a shopping bag she'd brought and pulled out five clean white robes and five pairs of sandals.

"Fresh clothes, godlings!" She began handing out the robes and footgear.

The sandals and the robes were way too big. But Mom said that if we always ate everything on our plates, we'd soon grow into them.

We sat down in the shade of an olive tree then, and had our first picnic. Mom was too big to sit under the tree, but she sat close by. She'd brought a basket of yummy ambrosia sandwiches and nectar punch for our lunch.

"Eat all your ambrosia," Mom told us. "That's what makes healthy ichor flow through your godling veins."

Ichor—that's what we gods have instead of blood.

We all dug in. It was a long, slow feast. Demeter ran up the hill every once in a while to check on Dad, but he was out cold.

"Now," said Mom, when we'd finished eating, "let me tell you how you came to be rescued."

"We know that already, Mother," Hera said. "Zeus told us how he put powerful herbs in Dad's tea."

Mom's eyebrows went up. "Zeus . . ." she said in a warning tone of voice.

"Okay, okay. *You* found the herbs," Zeus admitted.

"And who told Cronus that the herbs would make him unconquerable?" Mom asked. "Who gave them to Cronus to drink in an herbal nectar tea?"

"You did, Mom," Zeus muttered. "You did."

Mom shook her head. "What did those nymphs in that cave teach you, Zeusie? That it's all right to lie? To be a myth-o-maniac?"

"No!" cried Zeus. "I figured that out for myself!"

Mom took a deep breath. "Anyway, the main thing is that I have my godlings back!" And there was more hugging and kissing.

After that, Po talked everyone into taking another dip. But Mom waggled a finger at me. "Come here, Hades. I need a private word with you."

I felt very special with Mom singling me out this way. I sat back down under the olive tree next to her.

"Hades, my firstborn!" she said. "Let me tell you why your Daddy swallowed you godlings." And she told me about the old seer and his prophecy.

"He'll do anything to keep you kids from taking over," Mom said. "So it's important for the six of you to stick together and be on the look out for Cronus. You're the oldest, Hades, so you have some extra responsibilities."

Uh-oh. I didn't like the sound of that.

"I want you to keep an eye on the others," Mom went on. "Make sure they stay out of trouble."

"They won't listen to me, Mom!" I said. "Besides, they're all gods. They're immortal. Nothing can happen to them."

"Ha!" Mom said. "You don't know the ways of the world, Hades. There's plenty of mischief a young god can get into without half trying. Zeus in particular worries me. Those nymphs spoiled him terribly, and now he thinks he can get away with anything. And his myth-o-mania—" She shook her head. "That could get him into big trouble one day."

Just then Dad moaned. We saw that he had lifted his head.

"I have to scoot." Mom hopped up and started gathering her things. "I don't want to be around when Cronus remembers who gave him that tea."

"Bye, Mom," I said, hoping she'd forget about the responsibility thing.

I should have known better.

"Not so fast, Hades." Mom pawed around in that bag of hers again and took out a small vial. "This is filled with water from the River Styx in the Underworld."

I didn't have a clue what she was talking about.

"Put your left hand on the vial," Mom said. "Raise your right hand. Now swear an oath that you will look after your brothers and sisters, Hades. Especially Zeus. Make sure no harm comes to him."

I sighed. "All right. I swear."

Mom smiled. She tossed the vial back into her bag. "Oaths sworn on the River Styx are unbreakable, you know." She began to glow.

"They are?" I said. Her glow grew brighter and brighter. "You mean for my whole, long, eternal life I'm doomed to—"

"Ta-ta, Hades!" Mom cut in. "Tell the others good-bye for me, will you? I'll be in touch!" Then her glow went into hyperdrive, and *ZIP!* She was gone.

## Chapter III

# HE'S TOAST!

Dad was waking up, and gone seemed like a good place to be. I ran over to the stream to warn the others. Po was holding some sort of class.

"Run in place!" Po instructed. "Knees high!" He waved to me. "I call this water aerobics, Hades!" he shouted. "Come on, Zeus! Get your heart rate up!"

"We're immortal, you ninny," Zeus growled. "We don't have to exercise!"

"Dad's waking up!" I called.

My sibs stopped running in place and ran for real to the shore. They threw on their robes.

"Let's get out of here!" cried Zeus. "We can hide in my old cave!"

"Wait!" I said. "I have an idea."

"Make it quick, Hades," Hera said. "I, for one, have no wish to get swallowed up again."

"Quick?" I said. "Okay. An old seer told Dad that one of us will be mightier than he is. That's why he swallowed us in the first place, and why he'll never leave us alone. He'll keep trying to catch us and swallow us again or lock us up to make sure we don't overthrow him."

Zeus scratched his head. "What are you getting at, Hades?"

"That maybe we should go after Dad now, and try to overthrow him while he's weak and sick."

"Fat chance!" said Po.

"He'll swallow us again!" Demeter added.

"To my cave!" cried Zeus.

"Wait!" said Hera. "Hades is right. Once Father starts to feel better, we'll never be able to overpower him. But if we strike now, we might have a chance."

"Last one to Dad is a rotten egg!" said Po.

And we charged up the hill.

Dad had managed to push himself up to a sitting position. But he swayed as he sat, looking none too steady. His eyes were half closed. His face was red and blotchy. His mouth hung open. He smelled so awful that, without saying a word, the six of us shifted as we ran so that we approached him from upwind.

Dad's eyes were half closed, as I said, but they were half open, too. He saw us coming. He reached for his silver sickle.

"Be gone, spawn!" he growled.

"You won't be rid of us that easily, Father!" cried Hera.

"Shhh!" Dad said. "Not so loud. Ooooh, my pounding head."

"LOUD?" I yelled. "WE CAN DO LOUD!"

We all began yelling and shouting. Zeus banged his sword on his aegis.

Dad put his hands over his ears. "Have mercy!" he cried.

"Why should we?" shouted Po. "You're a bad dad! All those years we spent trapped down in your belly, did you show us any mercy?"

"NO!" the five of us shouted.

And with that we all began running around him, whooping and shouting and making as much noise as possible. Zeus kept up his banging.

Dad groaned and struggled to his feet. He flung his sickle at Zeus. It hit the aegis, and bounced off.

"Nonny, nonny, nee-jus! You can't pierce my aegis!" chanted Zeus.

Demeter quickly bent down and picked up the sickle. She held it up over her head. "I shall use this to harvest wheat!"

"Stay on task, Demeter!" scolded Hera.

"Uh . . . sorry," mumbled Demeter.

Zeus grabbed the sickle from her. He waved it in the air. "I am mightier than mighty Cronus now!"

"No one is mightier than mighty Cronus!" Dad roared. He lunged at Zeus.

"Yikes!" Zeus cried, jumping out of the way.

And before Dad could catch himself, he tripped over the root of an olive tree and went tumbling down the hill.

The six of us ran to the edge of the hill and watched him as he rolled. Faster and faster he went, down, down, down. As he rolled, he picked up soil and gravel and even a bush or two. He went so fast that sparks began to fly, and near the bottom of the hill, the whole thing burst into flames. Seconds later, he splashed into the sea, steaming and hissing. Looking very much like a huge, smoking, cigar-shaped island, he drifted off toward a spit of land that we later learned was Italy.

"He's toast!" yelled Zeus.

"Bye-bye, big, bad Dad!" called Po.

"So long, Age of Titans!" called Hestia. "Hello, Age of Godlings!"

"Not godlings." Hera frowned. "We need a name as strong as *Titan*."

"I think I've got one," said Po. "Aqua Gods!"

"Don't try to think, Po," said Hera. "Leave that to me. Now, we need to get organized. Zeus, the first thing you have to do is—"

Suddenly the ground beneath our feet began to shake. I grabbed on to the nearest olive tree and held on tight. Those who didn't grab on to anything got bounced all over the place. It was an earthquake!

After a while the quaking stopped and we all looked around. No one was hurt, so at the time we didn't think too much about that quake. Or wonder why Mother Earth, our own Granny Gaia, might be trying to shake us up.

# Chapter IV

## SUN SPOT

"I know this great place where we can live," Zeus said.

"It's not your cave, is it, Zeus?" asked Hestia. "Because Dad's stomach was like a great big cave, and we're sick of caves."

"We want fresh air and sunshine—and soil!" cried Demeter.

"And privacy," said Hera. "No more living on top of one another."

"Something with a water view," said Po.

"Mount Olympus has it all," Zeus said. "Dad used to live there."

"So why did he move?" asked Hestia.

"Maybe he got sick of the commute down to Greece every day." Zeus shrugged. "It *is* sort of a hike. But it's not hard for me. I've moved into Dad's old palace. The chairs and tables were titanic, but I hired some Carpentry Nymphs to saw them down to size. I look really cool sitting on Dad's old throne. Come on! I'll show you. And you can see the stable where I keep my winged steeds!"

So we trotted after Zeus, up hill and down, all across Greece. Demeter insisted on lugging the stone from Dad's belly, so she quickly fell behind the rest of us. After a while, the journey became mostly uphill and hardly any down. At last we found ourselves trekking straight up a mountain. The mountain was so high that the top of it was hidden in the clouds.

Zeus ran without breaking a *drosis* (old Greek-speak for "god sweat"), but the rest of us were huffing and puffing and drosissing like crazy. There hadn't exactly been a jogging track down in Dad's belly, and we five were sadly out of shape.

Finally, Hera yelled, "STOP!"

I, for one, was grateful. We all stood there, breathing hard until Demeter caught up with us. She was drenched in drosis.

"We're gods, Zeus," Hera said. "We have powers. There has to be a better way to get to a mountaintop than jogging up like mere mortals."

"Oh, you want to instantly transport yourselves to the top of Mount Olympus?" asked Zeus.

"Take a wild guess," said Demeter. Dragging that stone halfway up the mountain had given her a scary, desperate look.

"Hey, no problem," said Zeus. "All you have to do is close your eyes and spin around one foot, chanting, 'Fee fie fo fum! Mount Olympus, here I come!'"

The five of us closed our eyes. We started spinning and chanting all together: "FEE FIE FO FUM! MOUNT OLYMPUS, HERE WE COME!"

I opened my eyes. I didn't see the top of Mount Olympus. I saw Zeus, doubled over laughing.

"Gotcha!" he cried, slapping his knee. "Fo fum! Oh, that was a good one!"

"Myth-o-maniac!" Demeter cried, raising the stone over her head as if she meant to hurl it.

"Hey, back off!" yelled Zeus. "Can't you take a joke?"

"Not really," said Demeter, but she lowered the stone.

"Sorry," Zeus muttered. "I don't know of any quick way to get there."

And so we hiked the rest of the way to the top of Mount Olympus.

When we got there, we saw that for once, Zeus hadn't been lying. Mount Olympus was as great as he'd said it would be, with acres and acres of rolling green hills, burbling brooks, and a clear, sparkling lake.

"Whoa!" said Po, looking around. "Great lake!"

"Home, sweet, home," said Hestia.

"I see the perfect spot for my palace," said Hera, never one to waste time simply admiring the scenery.

A Welcome Nymph flitted over to where we stood. "Welcome to Mount Olympus," she said "where there's never any wind, it only rains at night, and every day is sunny."

After all that time down in Dad's belly, we were ready for sunny. We'd have privacy, too. Mortals couldn't see what we were up to because the top of Mount Olympus was separated from the earth by a thick blanket of clouds.

"On top of the highest hill over there?" Zeus pointed to a compound of stone buildings. "That's my palace." He glanced at the setting sun. "The Kitchen Nymphs usually have supper ready about now."

"You'd better not be lying about that," Demeter said, and we godlings ran the rest of the way to the palace.

That night we feasted in the Great Hall, sitting together at a long table. There was plenty of ambrosia, and the nectar flowed freely. The palace was gigantic, with dozens of rooms, so we all slept over that night and for many nights to come. Dad's old home became our new home, and our lives quickly settled into a pattern. Each morning, five of us were awakened by: "WAH-HOOOOO!" Then *SPLASH!* as Po cannonballed into the lake for his morning skinny-dip. The rest of us threw on our robes and strolled to the Great Hall for the breakfast buffet. Ambrosia with melon, scrambled ambrosia,

ambrosia pancakes with maple-ambrosia syrup, and freshly squeezed nectar—what a spread! With all that good, fresh ambrosia and nectar, we godlings quickly grew into full-size gods and goddesses.

After breakfast, the six of us went our separate ways. Zeus liked to ride around in his storm chariot all day, lying and bragging about his great deeds to anyone who'd listen. He started wearing Dad's silver sickle on his girdle. I guess it made him feel big and powerful. Po liked to swim laps in the lake. Hera was always rushing off to supervise the construction of her palace. Hestia took over looking after Zeus's palace, making sure things ran smoothly. She could often be found sitting by the fireplace, making endless "to do" lists for the nymphs. Demeter, as you might have guessed, got into gardening, big time. She planted acres and acres of corn. But her crowning achievement was a rock garden, centered around the stone from Dad's belly.

Me? I took long walks beside the river. I sat on high hills and took in the scenery. I followed Mom's orders and checked on the others. But to tell you the truth, I grew restless up on Mount Olympus. The sameness—all sun and blue skies—made life a bit boring. Okay, I wouldn't have traded it for Dad's gut. But at least down there, you never knew when Dad might get the hiccups. Or when something might tickle him so he'd burst out with a big belly laugh and we'd get tossed around. Life back then had been unpredictable. It had kept us on our toes.

Zeus's bragging soon turned into a problem. We all learned to duck out of sight when we heard his steeds coming. He got very cranky if he couldn't boast a good part of each day, so he took to driving his storm chariot down to earth. Mortals are easily impressed, and this suited Zeus perfectly. He began staying down on earth for years at a stretch. After a while, rumors reached us that he'd gotten married. Then we heard that things hadn't worked out. Then we heard that he'd gotten married again, this time to a Titan. The next we heard, Zeus was engaged to a mortal. And then to someone else. Before long, we started hearing about Zeus's children. Lots of them were immortal, too, and he began sending them up to live on Mount Olympus.

Most of us didn't mind.

But Hera wasn't one bit happy about it.

## Chapter V

# FAMILY FIREWORKS

Athena was the first of Zeus's children to arrive. She came all decked out in a helmet and a shiny suit of armor. She'd hardly set her metal-clad foot on Mount Olympus when she announced that she was the Goddess of Wisdom.

Hera freaked out. "We don't divide up our powers like that," she told Athena sternly. "We all dabble in any area we want to. Including wisdom."

Athena's gray eyes flashed haughtily. "Let's just see what happens."

Next, Hermes flew up by means of his winged sandals and his winged helmet. He was small, and looked far younger than his years. And talk about sneaky! No sooner did Hermes arrive than things started to disappear. Little things at first: an urn, a goblet, Po's nose clips and goggles. Once, Hera discovered that her favorite girdle was missing. Then she spotted Hermes wearing it, and hit the ceiling. But Hermes just laughed and tossed the girdle back to her, and even Hera couldn't stay mad at the little thief for long. He was just too charming.

Golden-haired twins, Apollo and Artemis, came next. Apollo had a lyre made out of a tortoise shell slung over his shoulder, and from the moment he arrived, there was always music on Mount Olympus. Apollo was a mellow guy, which is why we were all caught by surprise when he began talking about how he saw himself as the future Sun God.

Apollo's twin sister, Artemis, had golden braids. She said this kept her hair out of the way when she shot her bow. Artemis was crazy about hunting. After a few days on Mount Olympus, she complained that there weren't enough unspoiled woods for her tastes, and she began slipping down to earth to go on boar and stag hunts.

Dionysus showed up next, toting seedling grapevines. He and Demeter bonded instantly over planting them. Before long there were grape arbors all over Mount Olympus, and Dionysus set himself up as the God of Wine.

Then Aphrodite appeared. She was flat-out gorgeous, so it was no surprise when she said she hoped to be the Goddess of Love and Beauty.

After a while, Zeus's children began coming in bunches. The three Seasons. The three Graces. All these kids with their big talk drove Hera wild. But she managed to cope until the day the nine Muses showed up.

"Hi! I'm Clio, Muse of History!" one sang out. "The wheel was invented in 32 B.C.—that's 'Before Cronus.'"

"Call me Terpsi!" another said. "Muse of the Dance." She did a few steps of what we would later come to call the polka.

"I'm Thalia!" said a third. "Muse of Comedy. Here's a good one. Why did the chicken cross the road?"

"To be sacrificed to the gods, of course," Hera said.

"Wrong!" said Thalia. "To get to the other side!"

All the other Muses cracked up.

But Hera was not amused. That night, she called a meeting of the "belly bunch," as Po called the five of us, in the Great Hall of the palace.

"Something has to be done about Zeus's brats," she said. "If they keep coming in these numbers, it'll get so crowded up here we'll all have to convert our palaces into high-rise condos. It isn't right. And they have all sorts of high-and-mighty ideas about being god of this and goddess of that. Especially that Athena. Goddess of Wisdom, indeed! Who do these kids think they are, anyway?"

"The children of Zeus!" boomed a voice from the doorway. We all turned, and there was Zeus, standing with his hands on his hips, grinning like a maniac.

"My children are gods," he said as he strode into the Great Hall. "They're family. They belong up here with us."

Hera sighed. "Have it your way, Zeus. But you'd better stick around and deal with them. You don't know what they're like, always squawking about who has power over what."

"I'll be here," Zeus declared. He marched to the head of the table and sat down. "I've been thinking about how we gods ought to rule the universe, and I've come up with a plan."

The fact that the universe had been doing just fine for thousands of years while he ran wild down on earth didn't seem to have occurred to Zeus.

"You're not talking dictatorship here, are you, Zeus?" asked Hera. "That was Father's thing, and it didn't work out too well."

"Not exactly." Zeus shrugged. "But somebody has to be CEO."

"C-E—what?" said Hestia.

Zeus grinned. "Chairgod of Everybody on Olympus."

I sat up straighter when I heard that. If anyone was going to be in charge, it should be me. I was the eldest, after all. And hadn't Mom asked me to keep an eye on the others? Plus I was thoughtful, kind, hardworking, that sort of thing. I felt I had CEO written all over me.

So it came as a nasty surprise that I wasn't the only one who felt this way.

"How do we pick the CEO?" asked Hera. "Because if it's organization you're looking for, I'm your goddess."

"What am I, diced clams?" said Po. "I can rule the universe PLUS the seas, lakes, rivers, streams, creeks, and puddles."

Hestia leaned over and whispered, "Those are *parts* of the universe, Po."

"No kidding?" said Po.

"I know you call me 'The Boss' behind my back," Hera added. "Make me CEO, and you can call me The Boss to my face!"

Hestia turned to Zeus. "I've been taking care of things the whole time you've been away. It seems to me that I'm already acting CEO."

"I *am* the firstborn," I put in. "That should count for something."

"I see the universe as a garden!" Demeter shouted out. "With me as the landscape architect!"

Zeus smiled. "I guess we'll have to put it to a vote."

"That won't work," Hera pointed out. "We'll each vote for ourselves."

"Then we'll need tiebreakers." Zeus cupped his hands to his mouth and shouted, "Kids! Time to vote!"

The rest of us watched in amazement as Zeus's children burst into the Great Hall. Athena, Hermes, Apollo, Artemis, Dionysus, Aphrodite, the Seasons, the Graces, the Muses—the whole pack showed up.

Hera gasped. "They must have been standing right outside the door. Just waiting to be called!"

The kids squeezed in at the long table.

Now I understood what Zeus had been doing down on earth. He hadn't just been fathering children. He'd been fathering VOTES! Ooh, why had I promised Mom to make sure nothing happened to him? I wanted to be the one to MAKE something happen to him. Something awful!

"Close your eyes and put your heads down on the table," said Zeus. "No peeking. I'm talking to you, Hermes. Okay, all for Zeus as Supreme Thunder God, Ruler of the Universe, Chairgod of—"

*CLANG! CLANG!*

A loud noise drowned out Zeus's voice. We raised our heads. There was more clanging and what sounded like battle cries. We jumped up and ran to the entrance of the Great Hall.

From there, we could see, marching up the mountain toward us, an army of giant Titan warriors! They shouted and beat their swords against their bronze breastplates.

And who was leading them?

You guessed it.

"Dad!" we all cried.

"That's right, you little ingrates!" Cronus roared. "Big Daddy's back!"

He thumped his breastplate with his fist. "I'm over my stomachache, and I'm here for revenge. Me and my army of one hundred Titan warriors are taking back Mount Olympus! Once more shall Mighty Cronus rule the universe!"

## Chapter VI

# HOTFOOTED GODS

"Back off, Titans!" cried Zeus. "Or we shall destroy you!"

"You tell 'em, Dad!" said Athena, her gray eyes flashing.

"*How* are we going to destroy them, Zeus?" said Hera. "Think about it! You're the only one of us who has a weapon!"

But Zeus kept on. "Mount Olympus is ours, now!" he shouted. He yanked the silver sickle off his girdle and waved it at Dad. He thumped his fist on his chest, but it didn't make the usual booming noise. Zeus looked down at his chest and gasped.

"Hey! Where's my aegis? My impenetrable shield? Hermes? HERMES!"

"Yo, Pops!" Hermes waved. He had the aegis buckled around his own scrawny chest.

Zeus looked back at the Titans. His eyes grew wide.

They were almost upon us now.

"Oops!" Zeus cried. He turned and started running. Athena was right behind him. The rest of us sped after them.

I'm not proud of this, but the truth is, we gods fled in terror. We ran helter-skelter down Mount Olympus. Except for Demeter, who made a little detour to her rock garden first to pick up her beloved stone.

As we ran, we gods heard big Titan feet pounding behind us. At last we broke through the blanket of clouds. We kept running until we reached level ground. Then we hotfooted it across Greece. Mortals stopped to stare openmouthed as we rushed by.

"Gods on the run," Hera said. "How embarrassing!"

"Mortals will stop sacrificing to us if they think we're scared," Hestia pointed out.

Hera waved to the mortals. "Just warming up for the big marathon!" she called to them.

I looked back over my shoulder. I didn't see any Titans. I didn't hear any battle cries. Or pounding feet.

"They've stopped chasing us," I called to the others. "I guess Dad just wanted to run us off Mount Olympus."

And so at last we stopped. We stood there, gasping for breath and wiping the drosis from our brows.

"Now Dad will move back into the palace," Zeus moaned. "It won't be mine anymore!"

"Win some, lose some," said Hera. "Come on. Let's find ourselves a roomy cave where we can hide for the night, just in case."

We hunted around and at last we found a cave beside a lake. It was big and deep, with lots of separate rooms. We scurried inside.

The next morning, I woke everyone up and asked them to meet outside the mouth of the cave.

When we were all gathered, I said, "We need to—"

"Yes!" cried Zeus, who never could stand to let

anyone else run a meeting. "We need to come up with a plan for taking Mount Olympus back from the Titans. Raise your hand if you have an idea."

Of course no hands went up.

"I was going to say," I continued, "we need to find a new place to live."

"No!" cried Zeus. "Mount Olympus is our home! We have to take it back. Think harder! How can two dozen gods defeat a hundred giant Titan warriors?"

"We could take turns smiting them with your sword, Dad," Athena said.

Zeus nodded. "Okay. That's a start. Anyone else?"

But no one else had any ideas about how to drive the Titans off Mount Olympus, or about finding a new place to live. So that cave became our home. Hera, who could put a positive spin on anything, started referring to it as "Headquarters."

Hermes's son, Pan, who lived on earth, heard about us holed up in that cave. He came to visit us one day, and stuck around. Pan was a pretty strange fellow. He had goat horns and ears and a little goatee. He had hooves and hairy goat legs, too, and a goat tail. And talk about nervous! One day Zeus dropped the silver sickle onto a stone. The clatter startled Pan, and he screamed.

Pan's scream was the loudest, most horrible sound that any of us had ever heard, and it scared the girdles off us. We jumped up and started running around, yelling and shouting, and no one knew what was going on. In short, we were in a *panic*. It took a long time for us to get used to Pan's crazy shouting.

Weeks went by. Zeus never stopped badgering us to think up a way to boot the Titans off Mount Olympus. But no one ever had any ideas.

And then one day Hera called us all together. "I have a plan," she said. "We can play games against the Titans for the right to live on Mount Olympus."

"What kind of games?" asked Apollo.

"All different kinds," said Hera. "Kickstone, for one."

"Kick *what*?" said Zeus.

"It's a game we used to play down in Dad's belly," I explained.

"We can run races, too," Hera said. "And have jumping contests and wrestling matches. Whoever wins the most games gets to live on Mount Olympus."

"But the Titans already live on Mount Olympus," I said. "Why would they agree to play?"

"Because games sound like fun," Hera said. "And because the Titans will think they're unbeatable."

"They probably *are* unbeatable," Hestia pointed out. "They're titanic!"

"Size won't matter in the games I make up," said Hera. "And besides, we're a talented bunch. Hades spent all his time down in Dad's belly jumping. Carrying that stone has given Demeter amazing upper-body strength. And Po is a great swimmer."

"Yes!" cried Po. "Plus I invented the doggie paddle, the frog kick, the swan dive, and the cannonball!"

"You mean you're going to make up games based on what we're good at?" I said.

"Exactly," said Hera. "And since we're playing for Mount Olympus, we'll call them . . . the Olympic Games."

"I'll do weight lifting," Zeus said. "I'm as strong as an ox. No, make that *ten* oxen."

Hera nodded. Then she turned to Hermes. "You can sell anybody anything. How about flying up to Mount Olympus and talking the Titans into this?"

"No problem." Hermes jumped into his winged sandals, put on his winged helmet and off he flew.

While we waited for Hermes to come back, we taught Zeus and his kids to play kickstone. We played game after game of it in a field not far from the cave. Apollo was a natural dribbler. Aphrodite had a kick like a mule. And Dionysus proved to be a fearless goalie. Nothing got by him. The Muses were duds on the field, but they discovered a talent for standing on the sidelines and inspiring some amazing plays. Hera watched everyone and made notes.

Two days later Hermes plopped right down in the middle of a game.

"We're on!" he said. "When the Titans stopped laughing, Cronus agreed to play games for Mount Olympus. He gave me a list of a few games the Titans want to play, too." He handed the list to Hera. "We're to meet them in Olympia Stadium a week from today."

Hera raised a megaphone to her lips. "Listen up, gods. Intensive training starts tomorrow at dawn. The games I've invented will use your strengths—"

"Hold it!" said Zeus. "Who made you team captain?"

Hera shot him a look.

"Uh, for Olympic team captain I appoint Hera!" Zeus said quickly.

Hera handed a list of her games to Hermes, and he flew it up to the Titans. Then she drew a chart with the events she'd made up so far on the wall of the cave.

| EVENT | GOD |
|---|---|
| Archery | Artemis |
| Badminton | Athena |
| Dog Paddle | Po |
| Goat-Footed Race | Pan |
| Kickstone | Team Gods |
| Long Jump | Hades |
| Rhythmic Gymnastics | The Muses |
| Synchronized Swimming | The Graces |
| Weeding | Demeter |
| Weight Lifting | Zeus |
| Wrestling | Hades |

"Now, wait a second," said Athena. "What's badminton?"

Hera smiled. "You'll love it."

## Chapter VII

# OLYMPIC TORCH

Zeus stared at the chart.

"Hades is in *two* events," he whined. "And I'm only in *one*?"

"The idea is to win, Zeus," said Hera. "And get Mount Olympus back."

Zeus muttered under his breath and stomped off. He didn't show up at a single practice all week. Hera threatened to take him out of Weight Lifting, but he wasn't worried. He was bigger than anyone else. He knew Hera couldn't replace him.

The three Graces spent hours in the water each day, practicing their synchronized-swimming routine.

By the time Hera said they could get out of the lake, their fingertips were as wrinkled as dried figs.

I practiced the long jump in the mornings. My best was 16.5 dekameters—not too shabby. In the afternoons, Po and I wrestled. I got better at both events.

The only dud on our team was Athena. She swung the badminton racket fiercely, but she just couldn't hit the birdie. And all that armor made it hard for her to run around the court. But Hera just kept saying, "You can do it, Athena!"

The morning of the games dawned. We put on our competition robes, lined up by height, and marched into Olympia. Hestia had the bright idea of running ahead of us carrying a lighted torch.

Outside the stadium, vendors hawked demi-robes with GODS RULE! printed across the chest. And others that said TITANS RULE!

The games made the headlines of the morning edition of the *Olympia Oracle*:

**OLYMPIC GAMES TO BE PLAYED IN OLYMPIA**
**Mayor says: Games are a fad. They'll never last!**

We made our entrance into the stadium with Hestia running, carrying the torch. Ahead of us, the place was packed. In those days, there was nothing mortals loved more than a good contest between immortals.

"Who we gonna beat?" yelled the muse Euterpe. "Who we gonna defeat?"

"The Titans!" the other Muses yelled back. "Yeah, the Titans!"

We paraded once around the stadium and sat down on our bench.

A Titan in a black-and-white-striped robe walked onto the field.

"That's Themis," Hestia told me. "You know, the one they call Justice? She's the referee."

"A Titan referee?" I said. "Oh, great. She'll be really fair."

Now the Titans marched into the stadium. The crowd roared.

It was hard not to notice that the Titans were titanic. Okay, we gods had grown up, but we still only came up to the average Titan's knee. How could I ever beat a Titan in the Long Jump?

The Titans sat down on their bench—and it

collapsed under their tremendous weight. The whole team ended up milling around on the sidelines.

Themis put two fingers in her mouth and gave a mighty whistle.

The fans quieted.

"The first event is Archery," Themis announced.

A pair of nymphs ran onto the field carrying a target and set it up.

Artemis and a Titan carried their bows and arrows onto the field.

The Titan strung his bow. He put in an arrow and shot it.

"Bull's-eye!" said Themis.

Now it was Artemis's turn. She pulled back her bow-string, and shot.

"Bull's-eye!" said Themis.

After a dozen perfect shots each, Themis made the archers back up. They still got bull's-eyes. Themis had them shoot standing on one foot. And then on the other. But it wasn't until she blindfolded them that the Titan shot an arrow just left of center.

"The gold medal for Archery goes to the gods!" Themis announced.

The mortals cheered as Artemis proudly took her medal.

The scoreboard showed one medal for the gods. And for the Titans? Zip.

"The next event is Badminton," called Themis.

Athena walked sullenly to the middle of the field, where the nymphs had laid out a badminton court.

Her Titan opponent threw the birdie up and slammed it over the net. Athena ducked. The birdie hit her armor and bounced off. The Muses tried, but they couldn't inspire Athena. In no time, Themis was handing the gold medal for Badminton to the Titans. Again, the mortals cheered.

Now each team had one gold medal.

After that, the Muses won Rhythmic Gymnastics, no drosis, and we pulled ahead. Then the Titan Ocean killed Po in the Doggie Paddle. Tied again. Demeter cleaned up in the Weeding event, which put us up by one. Next came Weight Lifting.

The Titan went first. Then Zeus stepped up to a barbell.

"You call these weights?" Zeus laughed. "I call them baby rattles!"

He put his hands around the bar and gave a mighty tug. The barbell didn't budge. He tugged again. And again. He grunted and made awful growling noises. But he couldn't lift the barbell off the ground.

"The gold medal for Weight Lifting goes to the Titans," Themis said.

"Strong as ten oxen, huh?" Hera said when Zeus came back to the bench. "You and your myth-o-mania!"

"Aw, that thing was nailed to the ground," Zeus said.

The score was tied again.

The games went on for days. The Titans took Breath Holding—an event they'd made up to draw on their titanic lung power. Then Pan medaled in the Goat-Footed Race. I got pinned in Wrestling, but Hermes cleaned up in the Frisbeus Throw. Dad had made up an event called Push Me. Contestants stood on a greased iron disk and challenged anyone to push them off. It was a crowd-pleaser, and it put the Titans one medal ahead. Then Po medaled in High-Board Belly Flop.

The score was tied again. And so it went. We'd win a medal, then the Titans would win one. Neither team could pull ahead. At last, with only two events left, the score was: Titans: XXXVI gold medals, Gods: XXXV gold medals.

"The next event is the Long Jump!" said Themis.

I started drosissing as I ran over to the sandpit. If I lost this event, we'd lose the Olympics! And how could I win against a Titan jumper?

Then I saw my Titan opponent.

"Dad!" I said.

Dad sneered. "Give up now, Hades."

I ignored him and stepped to the starting line. I took a deep breath and started running. I hit the toe mark and leaped into the air. I landed, pitching myself forward. I held still while the Measuring Nymphs ran out to see how far I'd jumped.

"Nineteen dekameters!" a nymph announced.

My best jump yet!

But Dad burst out laughing. "Nineteen?" he cried. "A *frog* can jump farther than nineteen!"

Dad kept laughing as the nymphs raked the sand. Then it was his turn. He stood in starting position. But he kept cracking up. He was laughing when he started running. He stepped on the toe line, still howling over my pitiful jump, and his foot slipped. That slip threw him off, and he lurched to the left. He jumped—a *lot* farther than nineteen dekameters—but he missed the sandpit entirely.

"The gold medal for Long Jump goes to the gods," said Themis.

"WHAT?" roared Dad. "I jumped ten times farther than he did!"

"That's true," said Themis, "but . . . "

"Re-jump!" cried Cronus. "I demand a re-jump!"

"Uh . . . that seems fair," said Themis. "Okay with you, Hades?"

"No!" I said. "I won!"

"Keep the medal, Hades!" Hera yelled. "Don't let them cheat you!"

I held tight to that medal. The score was tied again, XXXVI medals each.

Dad gave me a terrible look. "You'll pay for this, shortie," he said. Then he turned and strode off the field.

## Chapter VIII

# BRIGHT IDEA

"The last Olympic event is Kickstone," Themis announced. "If the score is tied at the end of the game, we will go into a sudden-death overtime. The first one to score wins the game. Okay, team captains to the field."

Hera jogged out to where Themis stood. Atlas, the biggest Titan of them all, did the same. Standing between the two Titans, Hera looked very small.

"We'll flip to see which team kicks off," said Themis. "Atlas, call it." She flipped a gold coin into the air.

"Gold coin!" called Atlas.

"She means call heads or tails," Hera said.

Themis flipped the coin again.

"Heads or tails!" Atlas called.

"Uh . . ." said Themis. "Atlas, your side can kick off."

I groaned. Themis was so unfair!

Both teams ran on to the field. I took up my defense position close to our goal. Themis put the stone down on the fifty-dekameter line. Our team backed up and got ready to receive the kick. Dad was kicking off for the Titans. He had a sneaky look on his face. What was he up to?

Themis gave a whistle, and the game began.

Hermes and Pan were too small to play kickstone, but they found ways to help. Pan kept score. And Hermes borrowed Hera's megaphone and set himself up as the announcer.

"The Titans are running for the stone, mortals," said Hermes. "Cronus kicks off! Ooh! The stone just missed the gods' goal. Now Dionysus picks it up. He kicks it to Aphrodite. She boots it to Apollo. Will you look at that god dribble? He's taking the stone deep into Titan territory. Now Cronus is—holy cow! He's pulled a sword out from under his robe! The other Titans are pulling out swords, too!"

So this is what Dad meant when he said I'd pay for winning the Long Jump! This wasn't kickstone. This was war!

"Cronus takes a swing at Apollo!" Hermes cried. "Apollo jumps back—he's safe! But the Titans have taken possession of the stone!"

Every time we got close to that stone, the Titans tried to whack us.

"Themis!" cried Zeus. "They're cheating! Call a foul! Do something!"

But Themis only shrugged. Titan Justice was no justice at all for the gods.

The score at the end of the first quarter was Titans: IX, Gods: I.

But we had a smart coach and we were fast learners. The next quarter, Zeus brought his sword onto the field, too. Apollo figured out how to duck under the Titan swords and keep dribbling. Aphrodite sharpened her aim. She knocked the sword out of many a Titan hand with a well-placed kick of the stone. Those of us on defense body-blocked dozens of near goals. By the end of the third quarter, we were only three points behind. And when the clock ran out on the game, the score was Titans: XXIV, Gods: XXIV. A tie!

Now the game went into sudden-death overtime. The first team to score would get to live on Mount Olympus—forever!

We gods redoubled our efforts. So did the Titans. We played all day. But we couldn't score on them, and they couldn't score on us.

At last the sun sank low in the sky, and it got too dark to see the stone. Themis whistled and declared the game over for the day.

"Report to the field tomorrow morning to finish the game," Themis said.

But the next day, neither team scored the final point. There was no score the following day, either. Days turned into weeks. Weeks turned into months, and still no one scored a point.

Mortals stopped coming to the stadium. You could pick up a GODS RULE demi-robe for next to nothing. And without the mortals there watching, the Titans played ugly. They started chopping down trees and flinging them at us. Whole forests quickly disappeared. When that didn't stop us, the Titans hacked boulders out of mountains and threw them at us. They ripped up the earth as the game raged on. But we gods gritted our teeth and kept playing. We didn't let them score.

Every evening, we retreated to our cave, bruised and ichoring. But every morning, we showed up at the stadium again. And so did the Titans. The game dragged on for ten long years.

Then one morning, Hera shouted the usual through her megaphone: "Up and at 'em, gods! We've got a game to win!"

And I knew I couldn't take another day of the kickstone war. I slipped out of the cave. I took off down the road. I didn't know where I was headed, but I kept walking for miles. The sun was blazing, and when I came to a stream, I sat down to cool my feet in the water.

I was so wrapped up in trying to think of some way to end the endless game that I never heard footsteps. The first I knew that I had company was when someone sat down next to me and put his feet into the stream. Big feet. Titanic.

I looked up and saw a Titan with blond hair and a blond beard. A pair of very cool blue sunglasses rested on top of his head.

"Howdy," he said.

*"What?"* I said.

"Say, you're one of those little gods, aren't you?" the Titan said. "The ones who gave ol' Cronus such a bad time."

I nodded, hoping he wasn't big on revenge. "Who are you?"

"Hyperion's my name," the Titan said. "And light's my game. You know Sun, Moon, and Dawn? They're my kids. A bright bunch, too. If only they'd take some responsibility! Most mornings, I have to drag Dawn out of bed and get her glowing. Sun always wants to stay up late. You should see what I go through to get him to set. And Moon?" He sighed. "She puts on weight, and then goes on a crash diet. Gets so thin you can hardly see her. Boy, howdy! Being in charge of light, day and night, can wear a fellow down."

"You don't talk like the other Titans," I said.

Hyperion nodded. "Don't rightly know why," he said, "but the day I bought me that cattle herd, I just up and started talking this way."

I didn't think I'd seen Hyperion around Olympia Stadium, but I had to ask. "Do you ever play in the Olympic games?"

"No, sir, I don't." Hyperion shook his head. "Cronus and those boys are a bad bunch. I hear they ran y'all off Mount Olympus."

I nodded. "If only we could win at Kickstone, we'd get it back."

Hyperion stroked his beard thoughtfully. "I know some fellows who just might help you beat those Titan thugs," he said at last.

I jumped up. "Will you come with me back to our cave—er, our headquarters—and tell that to all the other gods?"

Hyperion glanced at the sky. "I can't stay past sunset," he said. "So if we're going, let's skedaddle."

He led the way to an old flame-scarred chariot. We jumped in and he drove us back to the cave. We got there just as the rest of the gods were dragging home from another day at the stadium.

Hera saw us coming and shot me a nasty look for skipping the game.

I hopped out of the chariot and said, "Hera, this is Hyperion, Titan Ruler of Light. He's Dad's brother, but he doesn't like Dad any more than we do. And he has an idea about how we can get some help and win the Olympics."

"Announcement!" Hera called through her megaphone.

Everyone gathered round. Hera introduced Hyperion.

"Howdy," Hyperion said. "I'm thinking that my little brothers might like to play on your kickstone team."

"But you're a Titan," Hera said. "So your brothers are Titans, too."

"Not all of 'em," said Hyperion.

We looked pretty blank, so Hyperion explained: "After Mama Gaia gave birth to us Titans, she had triplets called the Cyclopes. Each Cyclops had one big eye in the middle of his forehead."

"Gross!" said Hestia.

"That's just what Sky Daddy said," Hyperion continued. "He thought the Cyclopes were beyond ugly. He couldn't stand the sight of 'em. But Mama Gaia loved her Cyclopes children. She kept saying, 'Sky Daddy, honey, they're family!' And Sky Daddy kept saying, 'Mama Gaia, honey, they're revolting.'

"In time, Mama Gaia had another set of triplets," Hyperion went on. "And this batch was *really* strange. Each one had fifty heads and one hundred arms. No kidding! Mama Gaia loved each little head, of course, but Sky Daddy? Uh-uh. He took one look at them and went, 'Yeeech!' He scooped them up, and the Cyclopes, too, and he flung them down into Tartarus, a deep, fiery pit in the Underworld."

"Wasn't Mama Gaia mad at Sky Daddy?" asked Demeter.

"You betcha." Hyperion nodded. "She was so mad that she helped Cronus overthrow Sky Daddy and she set him up as top Titan. After he took over, Cronus was supposed to spring the Cyclopes and the Hundred-Handed Ones from jail. He went down to Tartarus to get them, but he took one look at them and left them where they were. He was shaking-in-his-sandals scared they'd overpower him one day. So those ol' boys have been in jail all this time, locked up and guarded by Campe, the Underworld Jail Keep. They'd be mighty grateful for a rescue."

"But would it be fair to have them play on our team?" asked Hestia.

"Fair?" snapped Hera. "Are the Titans playing fair? I don't think so!"

"Rescuing those boys might not be any picnic," Hyperion added. "Campe is huge, second only in size to Typhon, the terrible donkey-headed monster. And I hear she has some ugly tricks up her sleeves. But, hey. It's worth a try."

Hyperion glanced up at the sun. He took his blue sunglasses from the top of his head and slid them on. "Duty calls," he said. "Good luck!"

Apollo ran quickly over to Hyperion's chariot and handed him the reins. It looked as if the wanna-be Sun God had found his role model. Hyperion clucked to his horses, and they galloped off toward the west.

"Okay! Let's get organized!" Hera said. "Hermes? Take a message to the Titans. Say we call a three-week time-out. Hades? You, Zeus, and Po go down to the Underworld and get the Cyclopes and Hundred-Handed Ones out of jail. The rest of us will stay here and—"

"Plant corn!" Demeter cried.

"Clean the cave!" Hestia said.

"Work on our kickstone skills," said Hera firmly.

Not one bit sorry to be missing that, I packed up a cooler of ambrosia sandwiches and Necta-Colas for the journey, then my brothers and I took off for the Underworld.

## Chapter IX

# HOT DOG!

After a nine-day hike, Zeus, Po, and I found ourselves standing on the banks of a dark Underworld river.

"This must be the River Styx," I said. "Mom told me about it."

"You mean the River Stinks," said Po.

"Pee-yew!" Zeus agreed.

The smell was strong, but to me it just smelled like an old auntie who'd put on too much perfume.

From where we stood on the riverbank, we could see the place where night met day. And one of the huge pillars, where the vault of the sky was anchored so that it bent over the earth in a perfect blue arc. The pillar was badly cracked.

An old boatman with a shaggy white beard poled toward us from the far shore. A sign on his boat read CHARON'S RIVER TAXI.

"Ahoy!" Charon called. "One-way or round-trip?"

"Round-trip!" Zeus called back.

"That'll be two gold coins," Charon said. "Each!"

"What?" Zeus cried. "Why, that's robbery!"

"If you're a living god, you can hand the coins directly to me," Charon said. "If you're a dead mortal, have a relative slip them under your tongue. I'll find them."

"We are immortal gods and we demand that you take us across!" Zeus boomed. "We aren't paying!"

"So stay put." Charon shrugged. "I don't care one way or the other."

Po eyed the river. "No way I'm swimming across this sludge."

As the three of us stood there trying to figure out what to do, I heard a growl. I turned and saw a little three-headed pup crouched down on the riverbank. All six of its glowing red eyes were fastened on Zeus.

"Beat it, dog!" Zeus said.

The dog growled louder.

"Scram! Vamoose!" Zeus kicked at the dog. "Begone, I say!"

"Hey! Take it easy, Zeus. This little guy is still a puppy." I squatted down and held out my hand. Instantly, the pup stopped growling and started sniffing me.

"That's a good pup." I patted his friendliest-looking head, and the other two heads started pushing in, trying to get some of the action. "Why, all he wants is love. Isn't that right, pup?" He wagged his tail.

"Lose the dog, Hades," Zeus said. "We're on a mission, here."

The pup pulled its lips back in a vicious triple snarl. He didn't like Zeus—obviously this pup was an excellent judge of character.

Zeus reached for the handle of the silver sickle that hung from his girdle.

I quickly scooped the pup up in my arms. All three of his tongues started licking my face like crazy. What a bath!

"Sorry, pup," I said, jogging away from Zeus.

"You'd better go back to wherever you came from. You don't want to stay around here, bothering Zeus. He's a little short on patience. Short on a lot of things, actually." I put the pup down. "Go on, now. I don't want you to get hurt."

The pup picked up a scent, and off he charged, one nose to the ground and two mouths howling.

I went back to my brothers, who had stepped into Charon's boat. Zeus was signing an I.O.U. He winked at me. I knew he had no intention of paying.

"This is a binding I.O.U. Signed while standing over the waters of the River Styx," Charon said while rolling up a piece of parchment and tucking it into his tunic.

"Yeah, whatever," said Zeus. "Just take us across."

After I hopped aboard, Charon did just that.

My brothers and I stepped out of the boat and onto the far shore. We found ourselves standing beneath a pair of bronze gates. The inscription on them read:

## WELCOME TO THE UNDERWORLD!
## MORTALS EVERYWHERE ARE DYING TO GET IN

We pushed open the gates and entered a gloomy

land lit by a mysterious silvery glow. Ghosts of the dead wandered aimlessly as far as the eye could see.

"You there!" Zeus called to a pair of them. "Which way to the jail?"

But the ghosts didn't answer. They glided by, talking to each other.

"*Epilogue*," the little ghost said.

"E-p-i . . ." The big ghost let out a moan. "Oh, I can't spell it! I don't even know what it means!"

"An epilogue is a short bit at the end of a book," the little ghost said. "It often deals with the future of the book's characters. Try it again. You can do it. *Epilogue*."

"The jail!" Zeus shouted at them. "Where's the jail?"

But the ghosts made no reply.

"I don't think they can hear us," I told Zeus.

And so we wandered aimlessly for a while ourselves. Zeus and Po complained the whole time.

"What a dreary swamp!" said Po.

"Disgusting!" said Zeus.

"There's no sunlight," I put in. "But it's not so bad."

When our stomachs started growling, we sat down under some black poplars and broke out the sandwiches and Necta-Colas.

A lone ghost wandered by, chanting, "I before E except after C. I before E except after C . . ."

I had just split my sandwich in two, and the smell of it seemed to attract the ghost. He came closer, and I held out half the sandwich to him.

The ghost took it and gobbled it greedily. A faint color rose to his cheeks.

On a hunch, I broke off another piece of my sandwich for him. He ate it and turned positively rosy.

"Do you know where the jail is?" I asked before he faded.

"East of Tartarus." The ghost pointed. "This side of the flames."

Then he drifted off, losing color as he went.

We ate quickly, then headed in the direction the ghost had pointed. We walked down a steep hill. The further we walked, the hotter it got. The sky overhead turned orange, reflecting the flames coming from the lower region. At last, we came to a tall stone structure built into the side of the hill. Its top was studded with nasty-looking spikes.

"This must be the place," said Zeus, wiping drosis from his brow. It was blazing hot in this part of the Underworld.

Sounds of hammering echoed from inside the building.

"And THAT must be Campe," said Po.

The Jail Keep of the Underworld sat on a stool just outside the great iron jailhouse door, fanning herself. She was huge, twice the size of a Titan. She had big hands and big feet. But for her size, she had a rather small knobby-looking head covered with thinning brown hair. Around her neck she wore a gold chain, and from her girdle hung a large brass ring with dozens of keys dangling from it.

Campe watched our approach with watery blue eyes.

Zeus put a hand to his chest, checking to make sure his aegis was in place. Then he drew the silver sickle from his girdle and cried, "We have come to rescue the Cyclopes and the Hundred-Handed Ones!"

## Chapter X

## SHINER AND CO.

Campe smiled. She was missing all but three of her teeth.

"Come to rescue them, have you now?" Her voice was deep and hoarse. Slowly, Campe stood up. She towered over us. "Well, come ahead."

"Hades! Po!" Zeus cried. "Charge her! I'll back you up!"

"Oh, puh-lease!" Campe laughed. She held up her key ring and jangled it. "I'll make you a deal. You can each take one shot at finding the key that fits the jailhouse lock. Pick the right one, and you can take my prisoners. But if you pick wrong . . . you're my new cleaning crew."

We eyed that jail. It was a pretty good bet that it had never been cleaned.

Campe held out the keys.

"Me first!" Zeus said. He took the ring and walked toward the door. He sorted through the keys, saying, "One potato, two potato, three potato, four." On "four," he chose a key, fitted it into the lock, and tried to turn it.

"Uh-oh," said Zeus.

"My turn!" said Po. He took the key ring from Zeus. He peered at the lock. Then he spread all the keys out on the ground and studied them for a long time. "Got it!" he said at last. He, too, fitted a key into the lock. But when he turned it, nothing happened.

I started drosissing. Now it was up to me to find the right key, or my brothers and I would end up scrubbing down the jailhouse—forever! I took the key ring. It weighed a ton. I examined the keys. They all looked the same. Then I thought, Campe opened the jail door all the time. She had to have a quick way to find the right key. An idea popped into my head. I took a chance.

"The key isn't on this ring, Campe," I said. "It's on the chain around your neck."

Campe smiled. "Well, well, well—a thinker." She drew the end of the chain out of her robe. Sure enough, dangling from it was a single golden key.

She put it into the lock.

*Click!*

She pulled the door open, and disappeared into the jail. We heard more clicking as she unlocked cell doors.

"Thunderer! Lightninger! Shiner!" she bellowed. "You've been sprung, Cyclopes!"

The hammering stopped. Heavy footsteps sounded and soon three giant Cyclopes appeared at the jailhouse door. They were as tall as Titans, but much skinnier. They stood looking out at us, each blinking one great eye.

Campe turned and went back into the jail.

"Fingers! Highfive! Lefty!" she called.

Again, we heard footsteps. Then a crowd appeared at the jailhouse door. It was really just the three Hundred-Handed Ones, but with fifty heads a piece, they looked like a crowd. These guys were even thinner than the Cyclopes. They, too, looked out at us questioningly.

"The little gods here have rescued you," Campe told them.

"Are you releasing us then?" asked a Cyclops.

Campe nodded.

"Let's pack up, bro's," said a Hundred-Handed One. "Don't run off, little gods. Be back in a flash."

They all ducked into the jail again, and we heard much banging and shuffling. A few minutes later, the six reappeared. The Cyclopes wore huge backpacks loaded with what looked like a blacksmith's forge and blacksmithing tools. The Hundred-Handed Ones carried small suitcases in many of their many hands.

"Drop me a postcard every now and then, boys," said Campe. "Let me know how you're getting on."

"Will do," said a Hundred-Handed One. "But what about you, Campe? You'll be lonely without us!"

"Oh, don't worry about me," Campe said with a grin. "This jail is never empty for long. Farewell, boys!"

With that, the nine of us started hiking. We were all glad to leave the flames of Tartarus behind.

We got to know our uncles pretty well on that trip up to earth. The Cyclopes were big, hairy, scruffy guys who smelled strongly of sheep. Thunderer and Lightninger didn't say much. But Shiner was a talker.

"We three are excellent blacksmiths," he told us. "We shall prove it to you when we reassemble our forge."

The Hundred-Handed Ones pretty much yakked nonstop. With one hundred and fifty heads among them, they could carry on up to seventy-five one-on-one conversations at a time. It turned out that Fingers, better known as Sticky Fingers, was an accomplished pickpocket. He managed to pick Charon's robe pocket when we crossed the Styx, then paid our fare with Charon's own gold coins. He gave him a handsome tip, too. Highfive was a famous prizefighter. And Lefty was an ace at throwing a fast-breaking curve-rock.

On the trip, we filled our uncles in on what was going on with the kickstone game. They promised to help us because we all had one important thing in common: we were all really, really, really mad at Cronus.

To our surprise, when we got back to the cave, Mom was there. Talk about a family reunion! She'd never met her non-Titan brothers before, and when your long-lost relatives each have fifty heads and a hundred arms, a simple kiss and a hug can take hours.

At last everyone settled down, and Mom brought out one of her amazing picnic lunches.

"Eat, eat, my long-lost brothers!" she said, beaming. She was never happier than when she was feeding her family.

Our weird uncles ate as though they hadn't eaten in centuries, which, in fact, they hadn't. Not ambrosia or nectar, anyway. Mom said this was why their immortal selves had shrunk down to nothing but derma and skeletos (old-speak for "skin and bones"). As they ate, our uncles grew bigger and healthier and stronger before our very eyes.

When we'd all eaten our fill, Hera stood. "I hate to bring this up," she said, "but we're due back on the field in Olympia Stadium tomorrow morning."

Shiner jumped to his feet. "Lightninger, arrange the tools!" he ordered. "Thunderer, commence reconstructing the forge!" He turned to Hera. "We shall create weapons and other items to assist you on and off the field!" And the Cyclopes got to work.

We gods spent the rest of the afternoon teaching the Hundred-Handed Ones the basics of kickstone.

As the sun went down, orange sparks from the Cyclopes' forge lit the sky. At last Shiner called, "We are prepared to bestow your gifts!"

We gathered around the forge.

"Time is scarce," Shiner began. "So we have made only three gifts. They are for the three gods who journeyed bravely to the Underworld to free us. Step forward, Zeus!"

Zeus did.

Thunderer held out a great bronze pail.

"A bucket?" Zeus cried. "What sort of a weapon is—"

"It is the Bucket o' Bolts," Shiner said.

Zeus reached into the bucket and drew out what looked like a long, zigzag spear. It gleamed with yellow light.

"Nothing can withstand the force of a thunderbolt," Shiner told Zeus. "Hurl it, and your enemies will experience dire consequences."

"Dire consequences," Zeus murmured, as he tested the weight and heft of his weapon. "Not sure what it means, but I like the sound of it."

"We Cyclopes swear by the waters of the River Styx," said Shiner, "that the Bucket o' Bolts shall never be empty."

"What do you say, Zeusie?" said Mom.

"Thank you, Uncle Shiner," said Zeus.

Shiner nodded. "Step forward, Poseidon!"

Po eagerly stepped up.

Lightninger handed him a large, three-pronged spear.

"No fair!" cried Po. "Zeus gets thunderbolts and I get a fish fork?"

"A trident," said Shiner. "A most powerful weapon. It can be hurled at your enemies or, for a more extreme effect, you may strike the earth with its shaft."

Po pounded the shaft of his trident on the ground.

Instantly the earth began to shake.

Po smiled. "Nice," he said. "Thanks, guys."

"Step forward, Hades!" said Shiner.

I did, although I had mixed feelings about getting

a weapon. I wasn't big on fighting. And so when Shiner held out my gift—a shiny iron-and-bronze helmet—I felt as if he'd been reading my mind.

"The Helmet of Darkness," Shiner said, setting it on my head. I was thinking what a nice snug fit it was when everyone started oohing and aahing and going, "Where's Hades?" and "What has befallen him?"

"Nothing has befallen me," I said to Shiner. "What are they talking about?"

"We can no longer see you," Shiner explained. "The Helmet of Darkness renders you, and all that you hold, invisible to gods and mortals alike."

I smiled a big invisible smile. For me, it was the perfect gift.

"All right, that's over with," Hera said testily. Her nose was out of joint because she hadn't gotten a gift. "Let's get a good night's rest. And tomorrow, we're going to win this game!"

The next morning, we put on our competition robes and lined up by height behind our uncles. Zeus and Po hid their weapons under their robes the way the Titans had. I hid my helmet inside my robe, too.

Off we marched for Olympia Stadium.

## Chapter XI

# T-BOLT ATTACK!

We marched into the stadium. The Titans were already on the field. We quickly jogged out and took our positions.

The Titans stared at our uncles in surprise.

"I know you," growled Cronus, eyeing Uncle Lefty.

"Yes, you do, bro," said Uncle Lefty. "You came to visit us in jail."

Cronus narrowed his eyes, trying to remember.

"You had vowed to release us from prison when you became Ruler of the Universe," Uncle Shiner reminded him. "But you broke that vow."

"You left us to rot in jail, brother," said Uncle Highfive.

At last the light dawned for Cronus. These were his ugly brothers that Sky Daddy had tossed down into Tartarus.

"Well, so what?" Cronus cried. "I'll toss you down to Tartarus myself when I'm finished with you here!" He turned to Themis. "Let's get started!"

Hera and Atlas jogged over to Themis.

"Hera, heads or tails?" asked Themis. She flipped the coin.

"Tails!" called Hera.

"What do you know?" said Themis. "It's heads."

As always, the Titans kicked off.

There weren't any fans around to hear a play-by-play, but Hermes took his place in the announcer's box anyway.

"The Titans will kick off," he said. "There they go! Cronus put some muscle into that kick. Nice stop by the gods' team. That Cyclops really kept his eye on the stone, folks! Now he's passed it to Aphrodite. She's dribbling toward the Titan goal. Intercept! Intercept! Titans gain possession! The stone is headed back toward the gods' goal. Atlas is lining up a shot. Oops! Another intercept! This time by a Hundred-Handed One. He's kicked the stone into the air. He's bounced it off one of his heads. Now off another. And another! Ow! That has to hurt! The stone is ricocheting from head to head while the Hundred-Handed One runs! He's taking the stone up the field. Amazing play here, just unbelievable!"

But every time we got close to the Titan goal, the Titans started uprooting trees and heaving them at us. They grabbed chunks of mountains and flung them at us, too. They did everything they could think of to keep us from scoring.

Now, on a signal from Hera, Po went into action.

"Po's pulled something out from under his robe!" announced Hermes. "It looks like a giant fish fork. He's pounding the earth with it. It's causing an earthquake! Everyone's falling down on the field. Po's down, too. He looks . . . shaken. Now the Titans are up again. They're taking the stone down the field."

Hera signaled me. I took out my secret weapon.

"Cronus is running at Zeus with his sword drawn!" cried Hermes. "Look out, Zeus! And—

what's this? Cronus's sword just flew out of his hand. And there goes Atlas's sword! What's going on, folks? Is there an invisible player on the field?"

Well, you know the answer to that one. I did what I could, but even with my best efforts, I couldn't grab all the Titans' swords fast enough.

Now Hera signaled Zeus.

"Still a scoreless game here in Olympia Stadium," said Hermes. "But wait. Zeus has just pulled something out from under *his* robe. Why, it looks like a bucket, folks. Now he's pulling something out of the bucket. It looks to be a thunderbolt. Yes! That's it! He's hurled it at Cronus! Whoa, is Zeus ever a lousy shot. That bolt is going to miss by a dekamile! Oh, no! It's headed right for my boy! He's hit! Pan's been hit on the hoof!"

"YAAAAAAA

AAAAAAAAHH!"

screamed Pan.

We gods had heard Pan shout before. But the Titans hadn't. They must have thought that the universe was coming to an end. They panicked, running in all directions, screaming and yelling, and smashing into each other.

Hera saw our chance.

"After them!" she shouted. "After them!"

# Chapter XII

## RED-HOT OLYMPIANS

We took off running after those panicked Titans. We chased them out of Olympia Stadium. We chased them across Greece. We chased them to the very edge of the earth, and all the way down to the Underworld.

The Titans were so big and they ran so fast that they didn't need Charon to ferry them across the Styx. In their panic, they leaped over the river. Campe stood on the far bank, waiting for them. The Cyclopes and the Hundred-Handed Ones quickly splashed across the river and helped her cuff the Titans.

Once the prisoners had been secured, Uncle

Shiner threw his arms around Campe. Thunderer and Lightninger did the same.

"How we have missed you!" the Cyclopes said.

"I've missed you, too," Campe said, patting their hairy backs.

The Hundred-Handed Ones got in on the act, then. All hundred and fifty mouths started saying how much they'd missed Campe, and all three hundred arms hugged her.

"Me, too," came her muffled voice from the center of the hug. "It's just not the same down here without you boys."

As we gods stood on the bank of the Styx, watching this odd reunion, I felt something cold and wet on my ankle. I looked down and saw a shiny wet doggy nose. Three of them, actually.

"Hey, there, little pup," I said, stooping down to pet his heads.

"Hold him there, Hades!" cried Zeus, pulling a bolt out of his bucket. "I'll zap him!"

"Back off, Zeus!" I reached down to pick up the pup, but he ran off on his own.

Zeus hurled a bolt at the dog as he ran, but I

deflected it with my helmet.

"Aw, Hades," Zeus whined. "You fun wrecker!"

Campe lined up her prisoners. "Titans!" she said. "Who is your leader?"

Cronus quickly pointed to Atlas. "He is!"

"I was kickstone team captain," Atlas admitted, "but technically, Cronus is—"

"The captain is in charge." Cronus folded his arms over his chest. "And Atlas was captain."

"What a slimy guy Dad is," Hestia said.

We all nodded in agreement. Zeus nodded, too, though it seemed to me there was quite a bit of Dad in Zeus.

"The way you played kickstone was a disgrace, Captain Atlas," said Campe. "All that hurling of trees and boulders. You cracked one of my sky pillars. Take a look at the sky, will you? It's tilting! Come over here." She beckoned to Atlas. "Now turn around. Back up, back up . . ."

She reached over and grabbed the top half of the cracked pillar. Grunting from the weight of it, Campe slid it over until it lay across Atlas's broad shoulders. She let go.

"Uggghhh!" said Atlas. "This is heavy!"

"Ought to be," said Campe. "It's the sky. This is what you get for playing dirty and breaking my pillar."

Campe turned and walked away, leaving Atlas holding the vault of the sky on his shoulders.

"Hey!" Atlas called after her. "Wait a second! How long do I have to hold this thing?"

"Oh, I'm thinking . . . forever," Campe answered. Then she led the rest of the Titan army off to Tartarus and the Underworld Jail.

We gods looked at each other. Only then did it dawn on us that the games with the Titans were finally over.

"We won!" said Zeus. "Mount Olympus is our turf again! We rule!"

We ran around slapping hands and hugging. We yelled, "What teamwork!" and "Together, we can do anything!"

I found Pan in the crowd. Some First-Aid Nymphs had wrapped his right hoof in bandages and said he'd be fine in a week or so. I thanked him, because without his yell, we'd still be up on earth playing an eternal game of kickstone.

"Announcement, gods!" Hera cried.

Everyone stopped talking.

"I've thought of a name for us," Hera said. "It's even stronger than *Titan*. No longer shall we be called godlings or gods. We won the Olympic Games, so henceforth, we shall be called the Olympians!"

We all clapped and cheered. The name fit. We were the Olympians!

"Mount Olympus, here we come!" said Zeus.

"Delay a moment, little gods!" Uncle Shiner called. He came splashing back across the Styx.

"No wading in the Styx!" Charon shouted at him. But he didn't try to stop him. He only poled his boat down river a bit, grumbling loudly about how hard it was for an honest river-taxi driver to make an honest living.

"We Cyclopes and Hundred-Handed Ones have made a momentous decision," Uncle Shiner told us. "We appreciate your rescuing us, and we are deliriously happy not to be in jail anymore. But in truth, we've missed Campe. And we've missed the Underworld. After inhabiting it for so many centuries, it feels like home. We've decided to stay."

We Olympians thanked our weird uncles and bid them good-bye. Then we made our way back up to earth. We felt great. With a little help from our uncles and a lot of help from Pan, we had defeated the Titans!

We hiked back to the base of Mount Olympus. We had just started up it when the ground began to shake beneath our feet.

"Po?" said Hera. "Are you doing that earthquake thing with your trident?"

"No!" said Po.

"Why does it always *do* this?" cried Demeter.

Now the earthquake started for real. This one was a hundred times worse than the last one. We were tossed and thrown around so much that by the time the quake was over, we were bruised and battered.

"Look!" cried Zeus. "I'm ichoring!"

Then the earth stopped shaking, and everything was still.

Too still.

I had a feeling that something BAD was about to happen.

Of course right then, I didn't have a clue how bad BAD could be.

# GREAT BALLS OF FIRE!

We hiked back to Mount Olympus and started climbing. It wasn't easy. But however bad it was for most of us, it was worse for Demeter, lugging that stone. I had to hand it to her. When it came to pure, dogged will, she had the rest of us beat cold.

"Are we there yet?" whined Po. He'd tried using his trident as a walking stick, but he kept causing minor earthquakes, so he'd had to stop.

"Shhh!" said Zeus. "What's that noise?"

We all listened.

"It sounds like wings flapping," said Hera.

The sky grew dark then, as if some gigantic

winged monster was flying past the sun, blotting out its light.

Which is exactly what it turned out to be.

We all stared in horror as the monster appeared above us in the sky. It had the head of a donkey. A mean, vicious donkey. It had a silver-scaled dragon's body. Its arms and legs ended in paws. Instead of claws, each paw sprouted huge writhing serpents.

"It's Typhon!" cried Hera. "That monster Hyperion told us about!"

Hissing and roaring, Typhon swooped down on us. Hot black smoke shot from his nostrils. As we coughed and sputtered, Typhon opened his mouth wide and spewed red hot lava down at us.

All the teamwork-bonding and the good togetherness feelings we had after we beat the Titans? Gone. Now it was every terrified Olympian for him—or herself. There wasn't even time to wonder why the monster was attacking us.

Before Typhon, none of us knew that we had the power to change ourselves into other life forms. But with red hot lava pouring down from the skies, our godly powers kicked into high gear. Hera instantly changed herself into a white cow and galloped off toward Egypt. (Leave it to Hera to turn into an animal that was worshiped there.) Apollo morphed into a crow and flapped off after her. Artemis became a wild cat; Aphrodite, a boar; and Dionysus, a goat. One by one, the Olympians all turned into beasts and ran away as fast as they could.

And the brave and mighty Zeus? Do you think he turned into a lion? A ram? A bull elephant maybe? Wrong, wrong, wrong! Zeus turned himself into a chipmunk, and dove down the nearest hole.

I didn't change into anything, but I did put on my helmet. Wouldn't you? Imagine that the world's biggest, meanest, lava-spewing-est monster was hot on your heels. A monster that makes Godzilla look as helpless as a day-old kitten! I think you'd put on the helmet, too.

Invisible, I dodged splashing lava as I ran over to the chipmunk hole.

"Zeus!" I called down the hole. "We have to drive Typhon away! He can't kill us, but if we get covered in lava, it will harden into rock, and we'll be stuck inside it *forever!* Forever is a long time, Zeus. Come out! We have to fight this monster!"

"Nothing doing," Zeus squeaked from inside the hole.

*BLAM!* A flaming lava blob hit the ground behind me.

When the coast was clear, Athena ran over to the chipmunk hole, too. She alone of the gods had bravely kept her form. She knelt down beside the hole.

"Dad?" she said. "You are *so* embarrassing!"

Zeus didn't say a word.

Typhon swooped down and wound his snaky coils around a great boulder. He flew up in the air with it and let it go.

*THUD!*

The boulder landed inches from Zeus's hiding hole, covering us with a thick cloud of dust. That was it for Athena. She quickly changed herself into an owl, hooted a farewell, and winged away.

As I watched her disappear into the distance, I heard that squeaky voice again, coming from the chipmunk hole: "Helmet."

I sighed. "Okay. I'll trade you my helmet for the Bucket o' Bolts." Zeus was useless in battle, so I figured it was up to me to get rid of Typhon.

Zeus stuck his little chipmunk nose up out of the

hole. I took off my helmet and put it down on top of the hole. It quickly rose up and vanished, and I knew that Zeus's invisible head was inside it. A few seconds later, the Bucket o' Bolts dropped mysteriously at my feet.

I gazed up at the sky. Where was Typhon? He wasn't circling overhead. Had he gone back to whatever deep crack in the universe he'd come from? That seemed too good to be true.

It was.

Typhon flew into view. His body was ten times the size it had been before! The bloated monster had flown to the sea and sucked up half an ocean. Now he blew it down at us in a terrible torrent. Zeus and I were caught in a swirling flood that swept us from the side of Mount Olympus. I couldn't see Zeus, but I heard him screaming.

I seized an uprooted tree and held on tight.

"Grab on, Zeus!" I cried.

"Got it!" came a disembodied voice.

Waves broke above our heads as the flood carried us out to sea. Typhon circled overhead. With one hand, I gripped that tree. With the other, I managed to grab a T-bolt from the bucket. I hurled it at Typhon.

*ZAP!*

The T-bolt bounced off the monster's leg.

Typhon howled in fury. He angled his wings for a dive.

I grabbed another T-bolt. I took aim at the creature's belly. I fired.

*BAM!* Got him!

A river of lava erupted from the monster's throat. Hot molten rock poured down on all sides of us, hissing horribly as it splashed into the water. But the great storming sea made us a moving target. Typhon never scored a direct hit.

At last our tree ran aground on an island that I later learned was Sicily. I ran frantically around the base of a huge mountain, looking for a crevice, a cave, any place to hide. I heard Zeus panting behind me.

Typhon flew after us. He hovered, getting ready to take a shot.

I quickly grabbed another T-bolt. I took aim.

*THWACK!*

"Take that, you fiend!" I cried.

The monster swayed crazily in the air, then plunged to earth. The ground shuddered as he hit. He lay still.

Typhon's eyes were closed. The monster was barely breathing.

"I think he's—" I began.

"Dead!" cried Zeus.

"I was thinking, hurt," I said.

But Zeus wasn't listening. He grabbed back his bucket. Then he ripped the Helmet of Darkness from his head. He tossed it in my direction, but it hit the ground before I could catch it. I picked it up and heard something rattle inside. I hoped it wasn't broken.

"T-bolts rule!" Zeus cried. "I have felled the mighty Typhon!" He strode over to the creature, and planted a foot on his back paw.

BIG mistake.

Typhon's serpent toes whipped themselves around Zeus, and faster than you can say *uh-oh*, he was caught in the monster's coils.

"Uh-oh," said Zeus. He dropped his Bucket o' Bolts. "Hey, let go!"

This capture seemed to revive Typhon completely. He managed a jagged-tooth smile.

"Not so tight!" Zeus gasped. "I can't breathe!"

Now Typhon let out what must have been a laugh. It bounced off the mountain, echoing in the air.

I jammed on the Helmet of Darkness and rushed to help Zeus. But when I came near, Typhon sensed my approach and spat a fireball my way.

Typhon held his captive up in the air. Quicker than a flash, his serpent fingers unhooked the silver sickle from Zeus's girdle. Then, with its needle-sharp tip, he began to pluck out Zeus's sinews.

Okay, raise your hand if you know what *sinews* are.

Take a wild guess.

Give up? No one who hasn't had the word assigned for a weekly vocabulary quiz has a clue what it means.

But here, take a crack at it. *Sinews* are:

a) bushy eyebrows
b) rotten molars
c) rubber-band-like things that connect your muscles to your bones
d) little prickly hairs on the back of your neck

If you picked c), bingo!

I know what you're thinking. Most monsters eat their victims. Or maybe they bounce them around for a while and *then* eat them. Or they breathe fire on them and toast them like marshmallows. But this sinews thing—that's a new one.

Well, Typhon had a thing for sinews. He pulled out every one of Zeus's. For a monster of his gigantic size, he had excellent small-motor skills. He threw the sinews into a bearskin bag, and drew the drawstring tight.

Without his sinews, Zeus couldn't move a muscle. His head slumped down on his chest. His arms hung limply at his sides. His feet swung in the breeze. He was as limp as a rag doll.

Satisfied with his work, Typhon hooked the sickle back on Zeus's girdle, and tucked the helpless Zeus under one arm. With the other arm, he scooped up the Bucket o' Bolts. Then, flapping his great wings, he rose into the air.

I could almost hear Zeus crying, "Help! Help!"

But without his jaw sinews, he couldn't even do that.

I stood watching Typhon soar over the mountain and bank to the right. Part of me, I'll admit it, was glad to see them go. Both of them—I was sick of Zeus!

But I heard Mom's voice inside my head: "Look after your brothers and sisters, Hades. Especially Zeus. Make sure no harm comes to him."

I'd sworn on the waters of the River Styx.

I didn't have much choice, did I?

It was up to me, Hades.

And so I took off in search of Typhon's lair.

## Chapter XIV

# FIRE ESCAPE

I ran after Typhon as he flew around the huge mountain. I saw that he was headed for a large cave just south of it. He flipped rag-doll Zeus over his shoulder and ducked into the cave. He called, "Honey, I'm home!"

I crept closer to the mouth of the cave. A terrible damp smell came from inside. I took a last breath of fresh air, and plunged in after Typhon.

In the dim light I spied a second monster. She was big, but nowhere near Typhon's size. Her body was that of a serpent, long, thick, and speckled. But she had the shoulders, arms, and head of a woman. A beautiful woman! Even in the dim light of the cave, I could tell that she was a knock-out. Six or seven junior monsters romped around her coiled body. One looked like a baby lion. Another had a girl's head on a winged lion's body. Still another seemed to be a goat with a lion's head. Definitely a strange brood.

Typhon hung Zeus neatly on a peg by the cave entrance. Then he tossed the bag of sinews to his wife. "Don't let this out of your sight, Echidna."

"As if I haven't got enough to do, tending our young," Echidna grumbled.

"Give me a break, Echidna," Typhon said. "Look! I've been hit by T-bolts!" He poked a serpent finger into a little hole in his gut.

"Ow!" he whimpered. "I'm going to Mount Nysa to see the Wound-tending Nymphs. I'll bet I need a tetanus shot." And with that, he ducked back out of the cave and flew away.

"The least little scratch and he's off to see those nymphs," Echidna muttered. "All right, kids," she said. "Nap time! Chimera, stop that butting. Sphinx, zip it up. I mean it. One more riddle, and you get a time-out."

At last the little ones settled down and snuggled up to their monstrous mama. Echidna sighed and closed her eyes.

Now was my chance to grab the bag of sinews. I edged invisibly toward Echidna. The bag rested against her shoulder. I reached out and took hold of it. Slowly, slowly I began to slide the bag away from her. I was patient. I took my time, keeping the bag moving almost imperceptibly along the cave floor.

Then suddenly, *WHAP!*

Something slammed into me. I pitched forward. The Helmet of Darkness flew off my head. Instantly, I became visible.

"Gotcha!" Echidna said. She wound her serpent's tail around me. "Name?"

"Hades," I managed.

"Hades." She picked me up and studied me with a pair of very pretty brown eyes. "I was just wondering what to have for lunch!"

I tried to smile, but Echidna wasn't so easily charmed. She began to put the squeeze on me. I couldn't breathe. And I shuddered to think that if she swallowed me, I'd spend eternity inside another gut.

Somewhere below, I heard dogs barking.

"Down, Cerberus!" Echidna ordered. "Be good, and I'll give you his bones to gnaw on."

But the barking didn't let up.

"What, Cerberus?" Echidna asked.

The barking took on a more frantic pitch.

"Cerberus," said Echidna, "are you trying to tell me that one day when you were playing on the bank of the River Styx, a mean god kicked at you and threatened to blast you with a thunderbolt and would have, too, only *this* god saved your life? *This* god? The one whom I am now squeezing so hard that his face is turning purple?"

"*YIP!*" answered the pup.

Echidna quickly set me down on the floor of the cave and began uncoiling her tail. As I fought to get my breath back, Cerberus ran over and began licking me with all three tongues.

"That was a close one, huh?" Echidna smiled, and her whole gorgeous face lit up. She picked up the bag of sinews and tossed it to me.

"Take it. And the guy on the peg, too. I don't know what Typhon was thinking, bringing him here. The last thing I need is another mouth to feed. Take your buddy and beat it before Typhon comes home."

I didn't have to be told twice. I quickly tied the bag of sinews onto my girdle. I scooped up my helmet, vowing to fasten on a chin strap so it could never fall off again. Then I ran over to Zeus. I jumped up on a table to reach him and lifted him off the hook. Oof! He was dead heavy. But I managed to hoist him over my shoulder the way Typhon had done. I jumped down from the table.

I took a quick look around for the Bucket o' Bolts, but it was nowhere to be seen. I gave Cerberus three fast pats on the heads. Then with a wave, I called, "Thanks, Echidna! I won't forget this!" and I rushed out of the cave.

I stopped for a second to put on the Helmet of Darkness. It sputtered, and I flickered from visibility to invisibility a few times before I disappeared for good. Then I toted Zeus to the seashore. Invisible as we were, it wasn't hard to catch a ride on a boat back to Greece, and from there I headed straight for Mount Olympus.

I carried Zeus the whole way up Mount

Olympus. I felt like Demeter, lugging that stone from Dad's belly. Only Zeus weighed about twenty times more than the stone.

I climbed until I reached the bank of clouds covering Mount Olympus. Then I took off the Helmet of Darkness to let the Cloud Nymphs see it was me, Hades. They quickly parted the clouds. I stepped out of them and onto Mount Olympus. Home at last!

Hera was the first to spot me. "Hades!" she cried, running to greet me. "Where have you been? Everyone was so worried!"

"It's a long story," I told her. I lowered the blob of jelly formerly known as Zeus to the ground.

"Aaaach!" Hera cried. "What happened to *him*?"

"A *very* long story," I said. "Help me with him, will you?"

Hera picked up Zeus's arms. I picked up his legs. Together we carried him to his palace. As we went, I told Hera all about Typhon, Echidna, and the sinews.

"Very strange," said Hera, shaking her head. "I'll call Hermes. He's clever. If anyone can put Zeus's sinews back in place, Hermes can."

We laid Zeus out on the dining table in the Great Hall. I opened the bearskin bag, and while I was taking out the sinews, Hermes showed up.

"Step aside," said Hermes, "and let me at him."

Hermes rolled up his sleeves and got to work. He managed to thread each of Zeus's sinews back into place, reconnecting muscle to bone. The only mistake he made was to start with Zeus's jaw sinews. Once they were reattached, Zeus could move his mouth again, and he began crying and screaming like the big baby he is.

By the time Hermes got Zeus up on his feet again, the sky overhead was growing dark.

"Can night have fallen so soon?" Hermes asked, glancing out at the sky.

Hera thumped an hourglass that stood nearby. "Has this thing stopped? It can't be this dark this early in the day."

That's when I started to get a bad feeling in my stomach.

## Chapter XV

### STAR WARS

I hurried to the door of the Great Hall and looked up at the darkening sky.

Typhon was circling overhead.

I groaned. Why hadn't I thought of this? Of course, Typhon would come looking for us!

The beast folded his great wings, preparing to dive.

"Zeus!" I yelled. "Get your storm chariot! We'll fight him in the sky!"

Zeus stood frozen to the spot. He had that chipmunk look in his eyes. I ran to him and grabbed him by the elbow. His muscles were weak from being de-sinewed, so he couldn't put up much of a fight. Still, he kicked and screamed as best he could while I pulled him to the stables. Hera and Hermes were two steps ahead of us. They'd already harnessed Zeus's steeds to his chariot.

I jumped in, and yanked Zeus in beside me. I picked up the reins. I gave those horses a slap, yelling, "Giddyap!"

The startled horses spread their wings and took off into the sky. In no time, we were high above Mount Olympus.

Then all of a sudden, *ZWACK!*

A thunderbolt whizzed by us.

"My T-bolts!" cried Zeus. "Typhon's got my T-bolts!"

The lightning flash startled the horses.

I pulled on the reins and cried, "Whoa, steeds!"

But they didn't whoa. In their panic, they raced up, up into the high heavens.

I heard Typhon's horrible growl behind us. I braced myself for another T-bolt. I wasn't disappointed. *ZWACK!* It came so close I heard my hair sizzle. The horses whinnied, winging their way higher and higher. Soon we were flying through the heavens, home to all the star-made creatures of the deep night sky.

Typhon raced on behind us, hurling T-bolts.

Suddenly, the Great Bear constellation rose up on his hind legs, furious at this invasion of his sky. Beside him, the Bull bellowed and pawed the air. The Ram lowered his head. The three charged Typhon.

But Typhon only grinned. He grabbed the Great Bear by one leg and hurled him across the sky. He drew back his arm and swatted the Bull as if he were a housefly. The Ram managed to butt Typhon, but Typhon grabbed him by the horns and drop-kicked him high into the stratosphere. All the while, Typhon kept up the barrage of thunderbolts, filling the sky with an awful flashing. Other star creatures panicked, galloping wildly in all directions.

Our only hope was to get the Bucket o' Bolts away from Typhon. I pulled at the reins with all my might, and at last regained control of the horses.

"Turn, mighty steeds!" I called. "Onward for the Olympians!" We began to circle Typhon then, going around behind him.

The horses obeyed. Closer and closer we came to the monster, speeding straight for his back.

"Zeus!" I cried. "See how Typhon is holding the bucket out with one arm? When I get close enough, grab it from him."

"Me?" cried Zeus. "Why me?"

I didn't bother to answer. It took all my effort to keep those horses on course. Closer we came, and closer still. The bucket was right before us.

"Ready, Zeus . . . NOW!"

Zeus made a halfhearted lunge for the bucket. He managed to knock it out of Typhon's snaky grasp, but he didn't manage to catch it.

The bucket spiraled through the sky, dropping down, down.

Typhon whirled around to see what had struck him. His huge face hovered before us like a giant donkey mask.

Typhon's snaky fingers reached out for us. If he caught us, I feared he would fling us into the outer skies, where we would orbit the earth for eternity.

But just before he grabbed us, the starry Goat butted in between his serpent fingers and our chariot. Caught on one of her horns was the handle of the Bucket o' Bolts. The Goat galloped close, then tilted her head, dropping the bucket onto Zeus's lap.

"I caught it!" cried Zeus.

"Start hurling!" I yelled. I wheeled the horses around for a frontal attack.

Zeus reached into the never-empty bucket, pulled out a bolt, and hurled it.

*PLIP!*

Typhon caught the T-bolt and flung it back at us.

*ZWACK!*

"We're hit!" cried Zeus.

The chariot swayed crazily. I glanced over my shoulder. The back half of the chariot had been vaporized.

The horses whinnied and broke into a wild gallop. I lost my grip on the reins. The horses headed down now, out of the starry heavens, past the moon, past Mount Olympus, through the clouds, down toward the earth.

Typhon flew after us, spitting burning hot lava at our backs.

The horses touched down in a field, never slowing for a second.

Behind us, Typhon hit the ground, too. He threw his long arms around a whole forest and uprooted it. He started hurling trees. We dodged one and then another as we galloped on. But it was only a matter of time before one of the huge timbers crashed down on our heads.

The terrified horses turned again and headed out to sea. We skimmed over the water. Our wheels touched down on the island of Sicily. We headed for the highest mountain on the island.

Typhon zoomed over our heads and landed in front of us. He opened his arms wide, encircling the entire mountain in his grip. Hugging it to him, Typhon gave a mighty pull. With a horrible sucking sound, the mountain came up out of the ground, trailing rocks and boulders.

Now Typhon threw back his head and let out a long, ichor-curdling laugh.

The awful sound panicked the horses. They bucked hard, snapping the reins and breaking free. They flew furiously away, leaving us sitting helplessly in the charred chariot.

Typhon raised the mountain over his head and hurled it at us.

"We're history!" whimpered Zeus.

In desperation, I plunged both hands into the Bucket o' Bolts. I grabbed as many bolts as I could and flung them with all my might at the hurtling mountain.

The bolts whizzed through the air and slammed into the mountain. Their force stopped it dead in its path. For a moment, the great mountain hovered in midair, frozen in space.

Then, with Typhon's laughter still echoing, the mountain began to fall back the way it had come.

*THUD!*

It slammed into the earth with tremendous force. It jolted us out of what was left of our chariot and sent us flying through the air. By the time we hit the ground, the earth had stopped shaking. All was still.

The silence was eerie.

"Typhon's a goner!" Zeus cried. "I did it!"

But I had an awful feeling that the battle wasn't over yet.

Then—*KABOOM!* The top of the mountain shot off. Red-hot lava and orange flames exploded into the sky. Thunderous roars came from deep down in the ground. The once peaceful mountain was now a raging volcano.

Zeus and I stood there, watching the fireworks. It was quite a show. After a long while, the fire didn't spurt so high. The roars quieted down. And at last the lava merely bubbled and boiled inside the mountain.

"He's toast!" said Zeus. "Typhon will never trouble us again!"

I had my doubts. After what I'd just seen, I thought Typhon might find a way to escape.

But to this day, he hasn't. Nope, Typhon is still trapped under that mountain, raging and roaring. If you don't believe me, go to Sicily yourself. Go to Mount Etna. You'll see a mountain belching smoke, fire, and molten lava.

Who else could it be under there but Typhon?

## Chapter XVI

# SMOKIN' GRANNY

"We have stopped the monster!" Zeus pro-
claimed.

"Right," I said, even though I didn't exactly agree
with his definition of the word *we*. My stomach was
growling like a beast. "So what do you say we head
back to Mount Olympus? Get cleaned up, and have
a bite to eat?"

Zeus only kept up his bragging. And his lying.
"I have felled the biggest monster ever! Never again
shall Typhon—"

But he said no more, for once again, the earth
beneath our feet began to tremble. The tremble

quickly turned into a major quake, throwing Zeus and me to the ground.

There weren't any trees to grab on to. Typhon had uprooted them all. So Zeus and I bounced around like corn in a popper while the earth bucked and cracked and seemed to change from solid to liquid form.

"Now what?" I moaned.

"NOW WHAT?" a voice boomed. "I'LL TELL YOU NOW WHAT!"

It wasn't Typhon's voice. It was a hundred times louder and scarier than that. Zeus and I looked around, expecting to see yet another monster with a grudge against us.

"Zeus? I don't see any monster," I said. "Do you?"

The shaking stopped suddenly.

"YOU CAN'T SEE ME," the voice boomed. "I'M TOO BIG FOR THAT."

Oh, great! A monster too big to be seen! This was curtains for sure. But somehow I managed to say, in the most respectful tone possible, "And who might you be, oh, mighty shaker of the ground?"

"I'M YOUR GRANNY!" the voice snapped. "GRANNY GAIA."

"Mother Earth Gaia?" I said.

"THAT'S ME," said Granny Gaia. "I'VE BEEN TRYING TO SHAKE YOU LITTLE GODS UP FOR A LONG TIME!"

"Like after we fought Dad?" asked Zeus.

"THAT WAS ME," said Granny. "I WAS ANGRY! HOW COULD YOU HAVE SHOVED MY SWEET LITTLE CRONUS OFF THAT HILL?"

"We didn't really shove him," I said. "He tripped over a root."

"SILENCE!" shouted Granny Gaia. "I'LL DO THE TALKING HERE. I AM NOT HAPPY WITH THE TWO OF YOU. NOT HAPPY AT ALL. LOOK WHAT YOU'VE DONE TO *ME*, MOTHER EARTH!"

She had a point. In the kickstone games against the Titans and in the battle with Typhon, many forests and mountains had been destroyed.

"But it wasn't our fault!" Zeus said. "It was Typhon's!"

"TYPHON!" wailed Granny Gaia. "OHHH! MY YOUNGEST! MY SWEET, PRECIOUS

DONKEY-HEADED BABY! PINNED UNDER THAT MOUNTAIN!"

Hyperion had been right. Mother Earth really did love all her children, no matter what they looked like.

"YOU'VE DONE AWFUL THINGS TO MY OFFSPRING!" Granny Gaia said. "NOW MY CRONUS AND MY OTHER TITAN CHILDREN ARE LOCKED UP IN THE UNDERWORLD JAIL!"

"But what about the Cyclopes and the Hundred-Handed Ones?" I asked quickly. "They're your children, too. And we got them *out* of jail."

"THAT'S TRUE," said Granny.

"And we're your grandchildren," I pointed out. "Most grannies are fond of their little grandkids."

"SO THEY ARE," Granny Gaia admitted. "WELL, MAYBE YOU'RE NOT SO BAD. BUT, THERE WILL BE NOTHING LEFT OF ME IF THIS FIGHTING KEEPS UP. I WANT PEACE NOW, DO YOU HEAR ME? YOU SIX CHILDREN OF CRONUS CAN BE IN CHARGE OF THINGS. I'LL DECLARE THIS

THE AGE OF THE OLYMPIANS. BUT YOU MUST RULE IN PEACE. GOT THAT?"

"No problem!" cried Zeus.

"HERE'S HOW IT WORKS," said Granny Gaia. "EACH OF YOU SHALL HAVE DOMINION OVER A CERTAIN AREA OF THE COSMOS."

She sounded like Zeus's children, wanting each god to be in charge of something.

"ONE OF YOU CAN BE GOD OF FRENCH FRIES, FOR ALL I CARE," Granny Gaia went on. "SOMEONE ELSE CAN BE THE GOD OF STANDARDIZED TESTING. YOU SIX GET TOGETHER AND FIGURE IT OUT. BUT NO FIGHTING. GOT THAT? NO MORE FIGHTING. AND, OF COURSE, ONE OF YOU WILL HAVE TO BE IN CHARGE OF IT ALL. YOU KNOW, BE THE RULER OF THE UNIVERSE?"

"No problem!" Zeus exclaimed again. His eyes gleamed as he turned to me. "Let's go tell the others!" And with that, he took off running.

"STOP!" ordered Granny.

Zeus stopped. "Huh?"

"HAVE YOU NO SENSE OF DIGNITY?" asked Granny.

Zeus shrugged. "Not that much, I guess."

Granny Gaia harrumphed. "I CAN'T HAVE THE GODS IN CHARGE OF THE UNIVERSE TROTTING AROUND THE EARTH LIKE A PACK OF WOLVES, CAN I?" she said. "LET ME TELL YOU A LITTLE SECRET."

And so it was that Granny Gaia told us how we could travel from one end of the universe to the other quicker than the blink of an eye. It's simple. I wish I could tell you how it works. But I can't reveal the secrets of the gods. If I did, mortals everywhere would be clogging up the skies, astro-traveling nonstop all over the globe. All I can say is that it does *not* involve spinning on one foot and chanting.

In any case, *ZIP!* Zeus and I found ourselves standing on top of Mount Olympus.

We quickly headed to the stables, where we were happy to see that Zeus's steeds had galloped safely back home. Then we went to Zeus's palace. I got cleaned up, and Zeus disappeared for a while. I hoped he was in the kitchen, letting the Cooking Nymphs know that fighting Typhon had given us a monstrous appetite.

In a while Zeus showed up and started banging his gong to summon everyone to a meeting in the Great Hall. All the other Olympians came running. We hadn't seen each other since most of them changed into animals and fled to Egypt, so there was a certain amount of hugging and slapping of backs.

After a while, Zeus's kids went off and Zeus, Hera, Po, Hestia, Demeter, and I took seats at the long table.

"Listen to me!" Zeus said to start the meeting. He began by telling everyone how we'd battled Typhon and trapped him under Mount Etna. The old myth-o-maniac took a lot more credit than he deserved, of course, but as he talked, the Kitchen Nymphs showed up bearing trays of ambrosia chips and ambrosia salsa and ice-cold mugs of foamy Nectar Lite beer, and I stopped listening. I only tuned in again when Zeus said, "Granny Gaia says we must choose one of the six of us to be the Ruler of the Universe."

I brushed the crumbs from my robe. I tried to look modest yet noble. Humble yet worthy. I felt sure that Zeus was going to announce to everyone that I, Hades, should rule the universe. After all, hadn't I risked my neck to save rag-doll Zeus from Typhon and Echidna's cave? Hadn't I hurled the T-bolts that pinned Typhon under the mountain? And I'd medaled in the Long Jump, fulfilling the prophecy that one of us would become mightier than Dad. In every way, I deserved the top spot.

"Voting won't work," said Hera.

"That's true," said Zeus.

"Whoever grows the best garden can rule!" said Demeter.

"But we have to choose now," Zeus said. "We can't wait until harvest."

"Pick me," said Po. "I'll be top god, no drosis."

"No volunteering," said Zeus.

"Then what do you suggest, Zeus?" asked Hestia.

A crafty look came over Zeus's face.

## Chapter XVII

# HAVE A HOT TIME, HADES!

It hit me then. Zeus had no intention of telling the others that I should be in charge. I had to speak up for myself! But as I opened my mouth, Zeus slapped a deck of cards onto the table.

"We'll play for it," he said. "Poker. The winner will be Ruler of the Universe. Second place will have charge of the seas. Third, fourth, fifth, and sixth places can pick whatever they want to rule on earth." He began shuffling. "I'll deal. Jokers are wild."

Zeus dealt. When I picked up my cards, I couldn't believe it. Not a single face card! Nothing but a smattering of threes, fives, and eights. I looked around the table. Hestia and Hera didn't look happy with their cards. Po and Demeter were scowling. Only Zeus eyed his cards with a satisfied smirk.

We anted up and started playing. The game didn't last long. When it came time to show our hands, the only one with any cards to speak of was—guess who?

Zeus spread out his hand. "Four aces!" he cried. "Yesss! I'm CEO, Ruler of the Universe!"

"I have four queens," said Hera. "I get the seas!"

"That is *so* not fair!" cried Po. "You don't have a clue about how to rule an ocean. Or a river. You don't even know how to swim."

Hera folded her arms across her chest. "I'll take lessons."

"Give me the seas, Hera!" Po begged. "Please! Pretty please with seaweed on top?"

"Yech," said Hera. "I hate seaweed."

"See?" cried Po. "I rest my case!"

"I have a full house," said Hestia, showing two jacks and three nines. "That makes me third. I want to be Goddess of the Hearth."

Hera narrowed her eyes. "What's a hearth?" she asked. "Is it better than the seas?"

"Much better," said Hestia. "A hearth is a fireplace. It's the center of every household in Greece." A dreamy look came into her eyes. "Just think of the burnt offerings and sacrifices I'll get every single night!"

"You take the seas, Po," said Hera.

"All right!" shouted Po.

"I'll be Goddess of the Hearth," said Hera.

"But that was *my* idea!" cried Hestia.

"So? I have a better hand than you do," said Hera. "I want the hearth!"

"I have clovers!" said Demeter, showing a hand full of clubs. "I shall be goddess of all things that grow from the earth!"

"Wait," said Hera. "Agriculture. That's big. Maybe I want that."

Demeter burst into tears then, and everyone started yelling and shouting at once. Hestia dumped a goblet of nectar onto Hera's head. Enraged, Hera started hurling ambrosia salsa at everyone, and Po started chanting, "Food fight! Food fight!" At that moment I was so sick of my brothers and sisters that my only wish was to get as far away from them as possible. And that's when it hit me. The perfect place for me to rule.

I stood up. I waited until the shouting died down.

"I have decided what realm I shall rule," I announced calmly.

"You can't have the seas!" said Po, and he, too, burst into tears.

"I don't want to rule the seas," I said. "I don't want to rule any part of the earth, either. I, Hades, shall rule the Underworld."

Everyone gasped.

"The Underworld?" Zeus's mouth dropped open in surprise. Obviously, he'd been afraid that I'd challenge him for Ruler of the Universe. Then he pulled himself together. "Wow, yeah, you do that, Hades. It's *perfect* for you!"

"It's settled then," I said. "I'm out of here."

"So long!" said Zeus. "Have a hot time, Hades!"

He was so eager that when he jumped up to hug me good-bye, three more aces fell out of his sleeve.

"Zeus! You cheated!" cried Hera. "We're playing again! I'm dealing!"

I closed my eyes and did what Granny Gaia

recommended for when a god wants to take a superfast trip from one place to another. But I went nowhere. And that's how I discovered that the Underworld is the only place in the universe that even a god can't *ZIP!* to.

So I took off walking, and nine days later, I found myself standing beside the River Styx. I took a deep breath. Ah! The air smelled sweet to me.

"Taxi!" I called to Charon.

As I waited for him to pole over, it occurred to me that living in the Underworld would be a little bit like living down in Dad's big, dark belly. It would feel like my first home. And I'd have my weird uncles, the Cyclopes and the Hundred-Handed Ones, to keep me company. Campe, too. I smiled. I knew I'd be happy here.

Once again, I heard dogs barking. I turned, and there was that little three-headed pup, racing toward me.

"Hey, Cerberus!" I said, giving him the old triple pat.

A rolled-up piece of parchment was stuck under one of his collars. I pulled it out and opened it.

Here's what it said:

**Dear Hades:**
**Cerberus has taken a mighty big liking
to you and wants to be your dog. He'll
make a first-rate guard dog of the Gates
of the Underworld, don't you think? I
know you'll take good care of my pup.**

**Best wishes,**

**Echidna**

The little triheaded pooch looked up at me with
all six eyes. His whole rear end was happily wagging
with his tail. I grinned. I had a kingdom. I had family
waiting for me down here. And now I had my very
own underdog. As Charon's river taxi nosed up to
the shore, I felt like the luckiest god in the universe.

"Ahoy!" called Charon. "One-way or round-trip?"

"One-way," I told him as Cerberus and I stepped
on board. "I'll be staying down here for a while."

## Epilogue

That's the real story of how Zeus became Ruler of the Universe. And of how I became King of the Underworld.

Not bad for a first book, was it?

After I finished it, I gave my ghost writers a couple weeks off. I spent that time thumbing through *The Big Fat Book of Greek Myths*, trying to decide which story to work on next. It was hard to decide. Zeus had mangled all the myths. There were so many choices!

One evening as I sat in the den reading, the door cracked open and Hyperion stuck his head in.

"Hey, ol' buddy," the Titan said. "Anybody home?"

"Come in, come in," I said.

Hyperion had retired, handing over his duties as Ruler of Light to Apollo and Artemis. He lived in the Underworld now, where the sun never shone. But he still wore his old blue sunglasses on top of his head. He grabbed a nectar brewski from the fridge, then plopped down opposite me in the big Titan-size chair I'd had made for him.

"Looks like I caught you with your nose in a book," Hyperion said.

"You did." I held up my copy of *The Big Fat Book of Greek Myths*. "Take a look, read it for yourself. You won't believe it."

One day Persephone, the goddess of spring, was picking flowers. Suddenly, the earth split open. Up from its depths sprang Hades, King of the

Underworld! He whipped his steeds toward Persephone, grabbed the maiden, and drove back into the earth, which sealed up behind him.

Hyperion whistled. "You did *that*?"

"No!" I said. "It never happened! That myth-o-maniac Zeus made it up just to make me look bad!"

Hyperion shook his head. "That ol' boy can really tell a whopper," he said. "But what really happened, Hades? How *did* you and Persephone come to get hitched?"

"It's a crazy story," I said, remembering. "You know, I've been trying to figure out which myth to rewrite for my next book, and I think that might be the one."

I smiled. "I think I'll call it *Phone Home, Persephone!*"

"Boy, howdy!" said Hyperion. "I can't wait to read it."

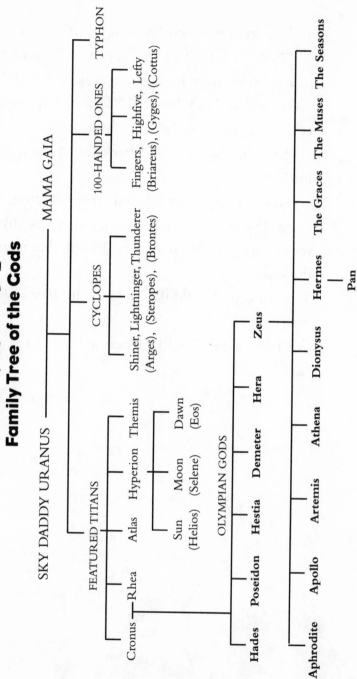

# King Hades's
# QUICK-AND-EASY
# Family Tree of the Gods

# King Hades's
## QUICK-AND-EASY
### Guide to the Myths

Let's face it, mortals. When you read the Greek myths, you sometimes run into long, unpronounceable names like *Aphrodite* and *Echidne*—names so long that just looking at them can give you a great big headache. Not only that, but sometimes you mortals call us by our Greek names, and other times by our Roman names. It can get pretty confusing. But never fear! I'm here to set you straight with my quick-and-easy guide to who's who and what's what in the myths.

**aegis** [EE-jis]: a magical shield or breastplate that no weapon can pierce; chickenhearted Zeus never leaves home without his.

**ambrosia** [am-BRO-zha]: food that we gods must eat to stay young and good-looking for eternity.

**Aphrodite** [af-ruh-DIE-tee]: goddess of love and beauty. The Romans call her **Venus**.

**Apollo** [uh-POL-oh]: god of light, music, and poetry; Artemis's twin brother. The Romans couldn't come up with anything better, so they call him **Apollo**, too.

**Ares** [AIR-eez]: god of war. The Romans call him **Mars**.

**Artemis** [AR-tuh-miss]: goddess of the hunt and the moon, Apollo's twin sister. The Romans call her **Diana**.

**Athena** [uh-THEE-nuh]: goddess of three w's: wisdom, weaving, and war. The Romans call her **Minerva**.

**Atlas** [AT-liss]: the biggest of the giant Titans; known for holding the sky on his shoulders.

**Campe** [CAM-pee]: giantess and Underworld Jail Keep.

**Cerberus** [SIR-buh-rus]: my fine, three-headed pooch, guard dog of the Underworld.

**Charon** [CARE-un]: river-taxi driver; ferries the living and the dead across the River Styx.

**Cronus** [CROW-nus]: my dad, a truly sneaky Titan, who once ruled the universe. The Romans called him **Saturn**.

**Cyclops** [SIGH-klops]: one-eyed giant. Light-ninger, Shiner, and Thunderer, children of Gaia and Uranus, and uncles to us gods, are three **cyclopes** [SIGH-klo-peez].

**Demeter** [duh-MEE-ter]: my sister, goddess of agriculture and total gardening nut. The Romans call her **Ceres**.

**Dionysus** [die-uh-NIE-sus]: god of wine and good-time party guy. The Romans call him **Bacchus**.

**drosis** [DRO-sis]: short for **theoexidrosis** [thee-oh-ex-ih-DRO-sis], old Greek-speak for "violent god sweat."

**Echidne** [eh-KID-nuh]: half lovely young woman, half spotted serpent; mate to Typhon, and mom to a strange brood of monsters, including my own underdog, Cerberus.

**Gaia** [GUY-uh]: Mother Earth, married to Uranus, Father Sky; mom to the Titans, Cyclopes, Hundred-Handed Ones, Typhon, and other giant monsters, and granny to us Olympian gods.

**Hades** [HEY-deez]: Ruler of the Underworld, Lord

of the Dead, King Hades, that's me. I'm also god of Wealth, owner of all the gold, silver, and precious jewels in the earth. The Romans call me **Pluto**.

**Hephaestus** [huh-FESS-tus]: lame god of the forge, metalworkers, jewelers, and blacksmiths. The Romans call him **Vulcan**.

**Hera** [HERE-uh]: my sister, Queen of the Olympians, goddess of marriage. The Romans call her **Juno**. I call her the Boss.

**Hermes** [HER-meez]: god of shepherds, travelers, inventors, merchants, business executives, gamblers, and thieves; messenger of the gods; escorts the ghosts of dead mortals down to the Underworld. The Romans call him **Mercury**.

**Hestia** [HESS-tee-uh]: my sister; goddess of the hearth; a real homebody. The Romans call her **Vesta**.

**Hundred-Handed Ones**: three oddball brothers—Fingers, Highfive, and Lefty—who each have fifty heads and one hundred hands; brothers of the Cyclopes and the Titans.

**Hyperion** [hi-PEER-ee-un]: a way-cool Titan dude,

once in charge of the sun and all the light in the universe. Now retired, he owns a cattle ranch in the Underworld. Has a taste for good books.

**ichor** [EYE-ker]: god blood.

**immortal**: a being, such as a god or possibly a monster, who will never die—like me.

**mortal**: a being who one day must die. I hate to be the one to break this to you, but *you* are a mortal.

**Mount Etna** [ET-nuh]: the highest active volcano in Europe, located in Sicily; beneath it lurks the fire breathing monster, Typhon.

**Mount Olympus** [oh-LIM-pess]: the highest mountain in Greece; its peak is home to all the major gods, except for my brother Po, and me.

**nectar** [NECK-ter]: what we gods like to drink; has properties that invigorate us and make us look good and feel godly.

**Pan**: god of woods, fields and mountains; has goat's horns, ears, legs, tail, and a goatee; his earsplitting yell can create a wild fear known as "panic."

**Poseidon** [po-SIGH-den]: my bro Po; god of the seas, rivers, lakes, and earthquakes; claims to have invented horses as well as the doggie paddle. The Romans call him **Neptune**.

**Rhea** [REE-uh]: Titaness, wife of Cronus, and mom to Po, Hestia, Demeter, Hera, Zeus, and me, Hades.

**Roman numerals**: what the ancients used instead of counting on their fingers. Makes you glad you live in the age of Arabic numerals and calculators, doesn't it?

| | | | | | |
|---|---|---|---|---|---|
| I | 1 | XI | 11 | XXX | 30 |
| II | 2 | XII | 12 | XL | 40 |
| III | 3 | XIII | 13 | L | 50 |
| IV | 4 | XIV | 14 | LX | 60 |
| V | 5 | XV | 15 | LXX | 70 |
| VI | 6 | XVI | 16 | LXXX | 80 |
| VII | 7 | XVII | 17 | XC | 90 |
| VIII | 8 | XVIII | 18 | C | 100 |
| IX | 9 | XIX | 19 | D | 500 |
| X | 10 | XX | 20 | M | 1000 |

**Tartarus** [TAR-tar-us]: the deepest pit in the Underworld and home of the Punishment Fields, where burning flames and red-hot lava eternally torment the ghosts of the wicked.

**Themis** [THAY-miss]: a Titaness, also called Justice, even when she's being unjust to us Olympian gods.

**trident** [TRY-dent]: a long-handled, three- pronged weapon made by the Cyclopes for Poseidon.

**Typhon** [TIE-fon]: an enormous, donkey-headed, fire-breathing monster with serpent fingers; now spends all of his time in Sicily.

**Underworld**: my very own kingdom, where the ghosts of dead mortals come to spend eternity.

**Uranus** [YOOR-uh-ness]: my grandpa, also known as Sky Daddy, first Ruler of the Universe; Gaia's husband, and dad to the Titans, Cyclopes, and Hundred-Handed Ones.

**Zeus** [ZOOSE]: rhymes with *goose*, which pretty much says it all; last, and definitely least, my little brother, a major myth-o-maniac and a cheater, who managed to set himself up as Ruler of the Universe. The Romans call him **Jupiter**.

Kate McMullan is the author of more than fifty books for children, including several collaborations with her husband, noted illustrator Jim McMullan. Their latest, *I Stink!*, stars a garbage truck with attitude.

Kate and her husband live in New York City and Sag Harbor with their daughter and their two mewses, George and Wendy.

Visit Kate at www.katemcmullan.com